I0746511

K.J.HERITAGE
INTERNATIONAL BESTSELLING AUTHOR

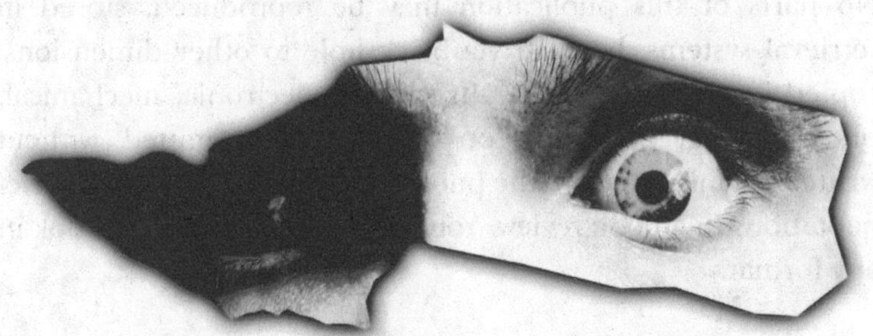

SHATTERED HELIX

Copyright © K.J.Heritage 2023

Shattered Helix

Published 2023 by Sygasm Publishing
All rights reserved.

Cover design: *K.J.Heritage*

No parts of this publication may be reproduced, stored in retrieval systems, beamed via black hole to other dimensions, copied in any form or by any means, electronic, mechanical, photocopying, recording or otherwise transmitted without written permission from the publisher except for the use of brief quotations in a book review. You must not circulate this book in any format.

Travelling back in time to publish this book before its official publication date is strictly prohibited.

All characters in this publication are fictitious and any resemblance to persons, living, dead, undead, existing in parallel dimensions or those having reached a higher plane to exist as intelligent corporeal gases, smells or colours, is purely coincidental.

Sygasm Publishing
http://sygasm.com

ISBN: 978-1-915927-98-9

For all the saps

"The best thing since Hugh Howie's *Wool!* Prepare to lose sleep reading *Shattered Helix!* Delicious Sci-Fiction!"
– Kate Danley, US TODAY bestselling author

"Gritty, intense, and compelling, *Shattered Helix* is something you don't run into often enough in Sci-Fi—a cerebral thrill ride you don't want to end."
– Michael Bunker, US TODAY Bestselling author of *Pennsylvania*

"K.J.Heritage's uncanny sense of pacing and story puts him at the forefront of today's speculative fiction writers."
- Samuel Peralta, Amazon bestselling author and creator of *The Future Chronicles*

"Gritty, detailed and unrelenting—*Shattered Helix* will take you on a wild ride."
- Peter Cawdron, International bestselling author of Science Fiction

What reviewers are saying about *SHATTERED HELIX*

"A page-turning burn of a read that has an irresistible hook at the end of almost every chapter." –Kip

"You won't put it down until you know the truth!" -Kay Boyle Smith

"…ingeniously thought out, with convincing characterisation and some wonderful touches of detail, brought in deftly enough not to slow down a taut and gripping narrative." -Makepeace McEvoy

"The twists come, fast and furious… a real 'who-done-it.'" -Rev Gurley

"…a thoroughly enjoyable read. I highly recommend it to anyone who enjoys both science fiction and murder mysteries." -BillieO

"...a tale of espionage to rival many greats in this particular genre… you certainly won't be disappointed." –Renee Spyrou

"A good fast read that will keep you on edge guessing!" -lcsdr60

"…an immensely entertaining story. Fast-paced doesn't adequately describe it." –Michelle Zeplin

"...thoroughly had me from beginning to end… Kudos to the author for writing such a wonderful story." –Dionne Washington

"From the intelligent, complex and likely half mad character that is Vatic, to a plot steeped with plenty of tradition." -Mark Rossiter

"I am not normally a sci-fi fan but K.J. Heritage has put it all together. It is exciting…with unique characters and enough space dust to track but not reveal the clues." -Denis E. McGrath

"The main character, Vatic, is wonderfully complex and his abilities are definitely cool." -Madam Ediotte

"Starts at a frenetic pace and the action doesn't really let up…a well written whodunnit set in space."

"You are a willing captive, unable to relinquish control until the very end of the journey... and then you want to relive the experience." -Selena Orseau

contents

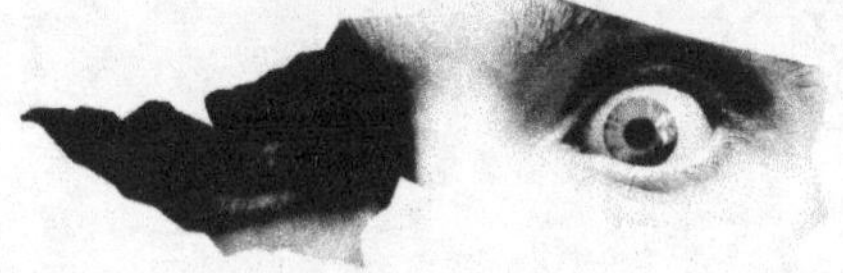

vatic

PAIN LIKE I've never felt before. Agony. Shuddering through me in wave after wave. I'm trapped under a great weight, unable to open my eyes, unable to move. Cold and shivering—frozen to the core. My legs and arms are twisted into tight knots, as if I'm rolled up into a ball, yet I'm lying flat, pushed down onto a hard, uneven surface stabbing into my back and spine.

I'm underwater—surrounded by a thick cloying liquid. Despite the freezing cold, my chest burns with a desperate need for oxygen. The sensation turns into a raging fire. My mouth bursts open and, like a dam riven by a series of underwater explosions, I'm coughing one lungful of fluid after another. The sound is muffled, distant—unconnected.

The crushing weight disappears, my face is uncovered and I snatch at the air, hacking and gasping. The cold recedes from my limbs, replaced by a slow warmth crawling through me with the sluggish thud, thud, thud of my heart. And with the pounding beat comes more agony. Every capillary in my skin stings like hot acid. Muscles pull against one other, dragging my joints apart. Tearing and snapping.

Something yanks at my head. My eyelids peel open. I see nothing more than vague blurs. I don't care—my ears are full of a lunatic's screams. A dreadful, screeching sound. With shock, I realise the screams are coming from my own throat. I try to close my mouth, yet the pain is too much. I scream again.

"For fuck's sake, shut him up!" The voice comes from everywhere and nowhere. A man. Gruff, unfeeling and urgent.

Another voice, by my ear. Female, strained and under pressure: "This will help."

A needle jabs me in the crease of my arm, releasing a heavy, soporific liquid that sprays into my heart and lurches down my arteries. Staunching the fire. Soothing my agonies. I relax, receding into a hypnotic haze.

I must've been in an accident—an accident I have no memory of. Everything is lost, even who I am. Only one image comes to me: I see a cheap hotel room with a viewing balcony. Stars hide behind a smoke-coloured fog, twinkling at me. Inside, stands a bed, the bedclothes tossed onto the floor. A black and white picture of a reclining woman with red lips is hung above. Sounds come from the bathroom. A female voice calling to me. And one other thing. I'm carrying a gun. I shake my head, trying to rid myself of the scene. I need to get away, to run—another needle stabs me in the neck and the memory fades.

"How is he?" asks the gruff voice.

"He'll live, if that's what you mean," the woman snaps back. "He was lucky. The Company writes in a ten percent wastage clause on all their hypersleep transports. The carriers see that as carte blanche to rid themselves of one-tenth of their passenger list just to save a few nutrients. His was one of the pods they switched off."

"And he's still alive?"

"Unbelievable, but we know what he is."

"So we did the creep a favour… shit."

"He's in a pretty bad way. Half starved. Nearly dead."

"That doesn't concern me. How long before you can get him on his feet?"

"A day or two. Three at the most."

"You've got thirty minutes. I want him up and alert."

The woman's voice is full of consternation. "Thirty minutes? But that means—"

"I'm not gonna tell you twice."

shots

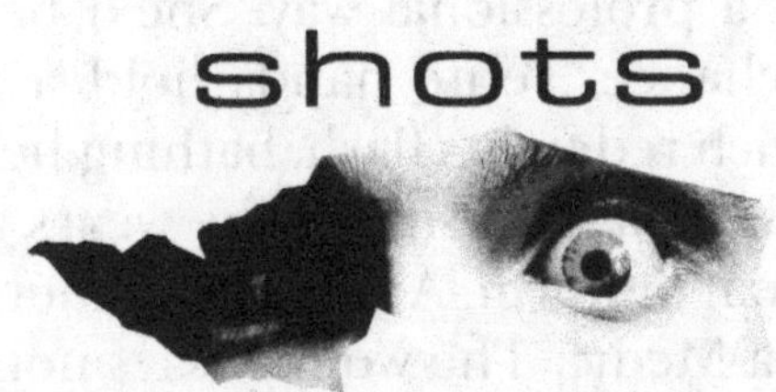

SOMETIME LATER, I'm sitting on the edge of a bunk in a small windowless chamber. It's functional, lacking any character. This must be the Medical Bay. The name is far grander than the actual room, which contains nothing more than a few cabinets and a sterilisation alcove. A couple of framed anatomical diagrams—reproductions—try to give the chamber a degree of gravitas, but fail miserably. Off-white paint peels from sagging metal walls held together by massive rivets and bolts. A single harsh light washes out all colour—not that there is any. A background hum suffuses the sound, almost like it's not there—a Matter Engine. I'm on a ship of some sort.

My mouth feels like a squad of shock-troops have used it for a toilet and my head is a screaming buzz gun, yet I'm over the worst of it.

A trolley full of syringes sits by my bunk, attended by the second voice: a worried looking woman in her late thirties. Ginger hair, dappled with the first hints of grey and out of condition from the recycled atmosphere, is pulled back from her face in a tight bun. Her skin is dry—flakes litter her forehead and cheeks. Large green eyes, slightly too wide apart, occasionally flick in my direction. Checking up on me, caring in a professional way. She'd be a looker given half a chance. Petite hands hold a flickering wafer from which red lights flash, bathing her features in crimson—like she's blushing. She wears a lab coat over a functional uniform. A crescent on her shoulder tells me she's a Medic. The woman says nothing, just grunts and curses. She's under duress, although I admire her manner. With a nod, she puts the wafer down and chooses the next syringe, the next shot.

I take the jab. This time deep into my neck. I feel the fluids enter me, can track them through my body. I can't tell what they're doing, yet the deep ache inhabiting my limbs reduces to a more acceptable level.

The Medic goes for another syringe.

I sit and watch, shivering and sweating—thin arms wrapped around myself like a child. Long, shaggy black hair encircles my shoulders and an immense beard tickles my chest. My legs shock me—nothing but skin and bone. I don't yet know who I am, but I remember my physicality. I'm not tall, though I've always taken care of myself. This body is starved. A pale imitation of what I once was. I feel genuine sadness at the loss.

And then a word: *Hypersleep*. I've been in hibernation. The word sparks other memories. *The Colonies*.

"I've pushed everything on a bit," says the Medic. "You may get the odd headache, but you should be starting to remember."

I stare at her. "Hibernation?" The simple effort of speaking tightens my throat and I start coughing again.

The barest of nods, her lips pressing together in a muted frown. "I brought you out fast and hard. Sorry for the rough ride. Orders." Her voice is typical of her profession. Curt and informative, yet softer than I expected. I sense anger and bitterness. She's been forced into this.

Finally, the dreadful hacking ceases. "Where the hell am I?"

"The Company. Where else?"

Thoughts race into my mind: anger, resentment and loathing. I can't remember who I am, but I know this organisation inside and out. "I hate the damn Company."

Her head tilts to one side, the frown turning into a grin. "Yeah, we all do. Lean back." The Medic pushes me down with a surprisingly strong hand. "You'd better hold still for this. The procedure isn't as bad as you may think."

I flatten myself on the hard bunk.

"Stare forward. First your left, then your right eye." She stands over me and brings up a syringe.

I grab her wrist. "Not in a million years!"

If she's scared, she doesn't show it. "You wanna go blind?" Her voice is as perfunctory as it ever has been.

"Don't ask me stupid questions."

"I've two grunts outside who will be more than happy to come and hold you down, or you can man-up and take your medicine. Your choice?"

The threat isn't an empty one—I believe she will do what she says, although her green eyes remind me this isn't her decision. The curt redhead isn't deliberately trying to hurt me. I let her go.

I don't feel anything as the needle enters my pupil. A quick squirt and she moves to the other eye. A stab of pain and a burst of mist that clears almost instantly.

"You dealt better with the procedure than I could. Then again… *you're Skilled.*"

The word is full of emphasis.

"There," she says. "You're done. Mostly."

I sit back up, blinded by my rough shock of untended hair. "I need a haircut."

The Medic's face comes to sudden life. "You sure do."

Creases appear around her lips. I sense she doesn't smile often—she seems almost embarrassed. It's now I notice the Triple Bar. Three horizontal lines sitting under the red crescent on her shoulder. "You're a Patron?" The Triple Bar is just about the highest rank in the medical profession.

"You're wondering why someone so highly qualified is stuck on a dumb ship like this? Mine is a long story. I won't bore you with it. You don't have the time. But it's because of me that we were ordered to pick you up. No one else was qualified to pull you out of Hypersleep."

I look around me. "You got anything to drink?"

"You've been given plenty of fluids, so you shouldn't be feeling thirsty."

"That's not what I meant, and you know it."

Metal rasping on metal and a man enters. I haven't seen him before, yet I recognise him. *The first voice*. It has to be. A thug resplendent in the light beige of the Company—the colours of all its personnel. An off-white typifying the organisation's true nature: faded, impure and stained. His rows of medal-braid are also worn, yet there is nothing pale about the man. Bearlike and animal, his hands like sledgehammers—full of power and purpose. A bastard with Company written all over him. I resent him before he speaks a single word. The Medic says nothing, although she shares my dislike. I feel the emotion stabbing out of her in a wave of loathing.

"I see you're starting to remember," the man says, his voice sharp like vinegar spat into the eyes. "I'm Strategist Stranng." He turns his attention to the Medic, his cheeks bulging with angry authority. "How is he?"

The redhead stares at her superior for a few moments. "Ready," she says. "Took a rough ride, but he handled the procedure."

The Strategist flicks a look of hatred in my direction. "It's his type. Can he handle the brief?"

A nod from the Medic. "His memories are still returning. But he's almost the real deal."

Stranng produces a wafer and passes it to me.

At first, I ignore him. Not wanting to look.

"Read the damn thing!" Stranng barks. "It's also your log for the mission. Data-tested and secure. Don't lose it."

I take the handheld off him. The wafer is as big as my hand. A screen from which my face floats in

3D. I know the photo is of me. *I just do.* Thick black hair, a grizzled chin, intense blue eyes staring back. *Staring into me.* High cheekbones and wide, pursed lips like some digivid of any half good-looking, thirty-something wannabee. I keep going back to those eyes. *My eyes.* There's something odd about them. Like I'm wired. Above this disturbing visage: one word: *Vatic.* The name scythes through me, releasing memories like the scatter of so many stun-gun pellets.

"I'm Vatic," I say, the croak of my voice less hollow, less painful.

"Yeah. That's you, all right. One of the Skilled. One of the Chosen—not that I'm a religious man. Far from it."

I try to give the wafer back to Stranng.

He thrusts out his lower jaw and sneers. "You deaf? The handheld is yours for the duration of the mission. Preloaded with everything you'll need to know. Or have you forgotten what you are?"

I want to speak again, but can only croak.

"And what on earth were you doing on a colony ship?" he barks, his grey eyes bright and challenging.

The question jars. "I… I wanted to start a plantation," I finally manage to spit out. "Away from all this shit." The statement sounds outlandish to my ears. A farmer is the polar-opposite of what I think I am. Yet, I remember the planet Jason. *A place of opportunity, of plenty and… escape.* Or so the datavids lied. "I have land waiting for me."

A snort. "Well get this, it turns out that until you put your feet on that poisonous dust-ball you were heading for, you're still owned by the Company. And it seems they have a job for you." He turned again to the Medic. "Kit him out in a skinsuit and bring him to the airlock." Stranng spins around and leaves the room.

I brush the hair away from my face. "Airlock?"

The redhead's green eyes narrow slightly. "There's been a death."

airlock

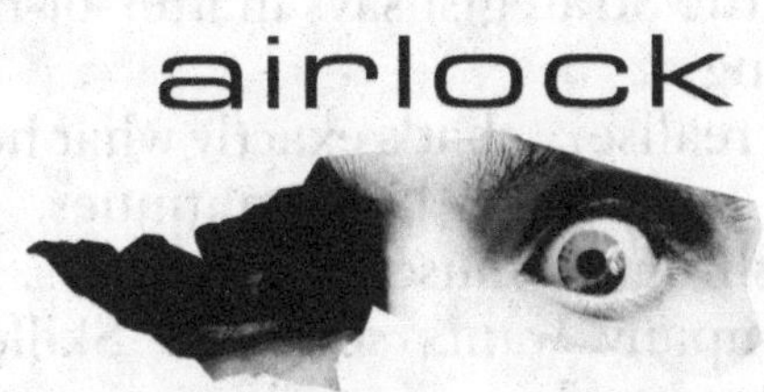

THE MEDIC pushes me through the ship, followed by two CPs—*Company Policemen*. Tight corridors stinking of sweat and piss. Gunmetal painted white. The floor is worn from the passing of many feet and stained with splashes of spilled coffee and space knows what other fluids. We walk past ship personnel. Nervous eyes dart at me—frightened eyes, worried. My attention is elsewhere—I'm trying to remember who and what I am. I wear a simple head-to-foot skinsuit tightly embracing my emaciated frame. Only my face is visible. My long hair and beard, still untrimmed, are tucked inside a tight hood. I feel safe, protected. But it's more than that—the skinsuit hugs my body in a familiar way.

Hydraulic doors clang shut and hiss open until I arrive at the cargo airlock. A dimly lit square of a room full of discarded equipment. Why have they brought me here?

Stranng arrives. The CPs salute, the Medic a moment behind them. She's purposely slow—disrespectful—and I'm liking her attitude. Stranng assesses the assembled bodies, taking the required number of seconds that authority dictates, and begins to speak. His eyes sparkling in the relative gloom as if powered by his own inner purpose. "Some scientist has wound up dead at one of the Company's secret laboratories," the Strategist says matter-of-factly, as if giving a briefing.

And then I realise… that's exactly what he's doing.

"Probably suicide," he continues. "Almost certainly." A shrug of muscled shoulders. "Not my call. The Company wants someone Skilled to go investigate—they've chosen you."

That word again. *Skilled.* I still have no idea what it means. I can't remember everything yet, although I feel a deep-seated resentment for the Company. "I won't do it," I croak through chapped lips.

"You think you've got a choice?" Strann nods to the Medic. "Tell him."

I've no idea why a Patron with a Triple Bar is stuck on this ship with brutes like this, but it can't be a picnic.

"You've got six hours, give or take," she says. "Six hours before your organs start giving up. You may last a further hour, if you're lucky."

"What the hell is this?"

Strann smirks. "An added incentive to get the job done."

The Medic continues. "The drugs I gave you, coupled with the accelerated process to bring you out of hypersleep, filled your system with toxins. Not even you can handle that amount of poison without a full blood scrub. I'm sorry."

Strann puts his face in front of mine. "A scrub we're withholding until you do what you're told to do… Unnerstand?"

I repeat the Medic's words in my head. *Even*

you can't handle that. There's something about me. Something special. And I've got six hours to find out what that is. Six hours to do this dumb job. "I'm an investigator?"

A nod from Stranng. "Of a sort." His mouth curls into a winner's smile. "If it was up to me, I'd have left you to rot in the hold of your colony ship. Only losers and fools trust the cargo-traffickers—you must have had quite some angle. Judging by the state of you, whatever it was backfired. And now you're here. Working for the Company again." The smile turns into a sneer of disgust. "And I thought we'd got rid of your type of scum a long time ago."

"He's not scum," says the Medic. "No matter what he's done, he's not that."

It's obvious Stranng is not used to being talked to in this way, but he says nothing. Somehow his silence is more threatening than a tirade.

The two-note of the intercom and an efficient voice: *"We are now in geo-synchronous orbit above the Karst asteroid, Strategist. We have a two-minute window."*

Stranng's sneer infects his whole face. "This ship is needed elsewhere, and we're late. I'll come back when we get the call from the Company—and not before. You're to meet with Director Anton Frederix, the stiff who runs the Zeta-Karst Laboratories. He'll brief you on the situation."

"Are they coming to pick me up?"

"Not as such. You're gonna have to find your own way there. You're about to take a little spacewalk. It's not far… just head for the nearest rock. That shouldn't be too hard for someone of your talent." He thrusts a facemask into my hands and stands back.

"Find my own way? I don't get it…"

"You've got six hours to solve this to the Company's satisfaction. Personally, I hope to never see you again.

And with that, the inner hatch opens and I'm pushed into the airlock, the door clanging shut behind me.

"What about my air!" I shout. "I've got no air!"

Stranng's face relaxes. He stares at me through the thick glass of the observation window, his eyes glittering as he hits the release button with a punch of his hand.

I have time enough to take a deep breath and attach my facemask before the outer hatch slides aside and I'm ejected into space.

torch

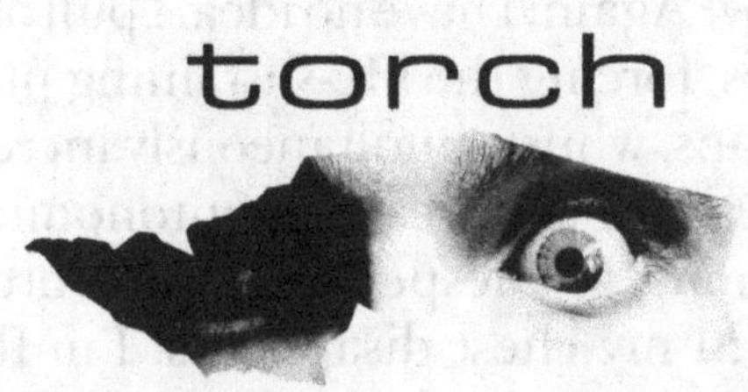

I'M SPINNING out of control. The skinsuit contracts around me, tightening—making it hard to move my limbs. I fight against the suit, against my predicament and by some means—space knows how—I stop my rotation. I'm protected from the harsh cold of space, but I've no oxygen.

No oxygen.

I grit my teeth and twist around to face the ship. The spacecraft recedes into the distance as I hurtle away. A typical Company vehicle. Featureless and empty of character. Made from block-like, yellow modules seemingly put together by an angry child. No name, just a number roughly painted on each of its many segments. A single, blackened matter engine sits underneath the enormous Snag Drive array—like the upturned crown of some ostentatious monarch. As I watch, the apparatus glows red, orange and white-hot—and the spacecraft is gone.

No oxygen.

I try not to think about the jam I'm in. About the pain burning in my chest. About how many seconds

I've got left before—

My heart slows. No, that's not right. I'm somehow decelerating its frantic beat to a sluggish, occasional thud. As to how? Again, I have no idea. I pull blood from my extremities, forcing the life-sustaining plasma into my major organs, whilst simultaneously increasing the flow to my brain. I suppress my autonomic nervous system, stemming my desperate urge to breathe and the tightness in my chest disappears. I'm floating in space, in a sea of rapidly diminishing oxygen, yet I'm surviving…

I spin again, turning towards the direction I'm falling. Hurtling towards an irregularly shaped asteroid, powdery grey and pockmarked with craters. I'm close enough to spot a cluster of buildings squatting on the surface, shining white like some forbidden temple complex picked out by a shaft of righteous sunlight. It's an illusion—the structures are the same dull grey as the asteroid. *The Zeta-Karst Laboratories.* I've seen hundreds of such constructions before—a Company installation. Also modular, built from identical pods and hemispheres of differing sizes. My destination. It must be.

This region of the galaxy is unnaturally dark. A far off star shines at the centre of this unknown solar system as a single, dim sun. It is accompanied by a myriad of tiny, half-visible stars—nothing more than white dots in the black, but I'm not alone. Another feature dominates the sky. An abnormally bright comet, with a short, iridescent tail, hangs upon the curtain of night as an immense, silent, glowing torch. I watch the blaze of searing white, mesmerised. The stark beauty is somehow calming. I can almost grab it with my hand and hold this torch aloft. And I'm suddenly a giant whose reach can stretch light-years. The scene is an illusion. The comet must be many thousands of miles away.

I have little time for contemplation. The asteroid grows quickly, and soon fills my vision. I bring my legs up, bracing for the impact. I hit the surface with a glancing blow. The skinsuit hardens instantaneously—intelligent nanofibres protecting me from the collision. I bounce once, twice, three times. The Company installation rears up in front of me. I scrabble for a handhold, but the suit is too stiff and I career, spinning, back into space. I twist around to once again face the asteroid and spy a figure in a powered skinsuit hurtling towards me. A hand grabs my ankle. I want to scream with relief, but I must hold on for a little longer. I'm not saved yet.

The figure, efficient and speedy, guides me down to one of the buildings. The red flash of an airlock and, within seconds, we're inside and the air is cycling.

karst

I LIE in the airlock, vomiting—or at least trying to. My gut has been empty since I entered hibernation, space knows how many years ago. Nutrients are no replacement for solid food in your mouth and stomach. I gasp, my lungs filling and emptying, heaving. The air is delicious, sweet. It has never tasted so good. I feel oxygen returning to my starved tissues—like waking up from hypersleep without the pain. My strength returns—what little is left of it. And there's something else. Whisky. I could kill for a whisky right now.

I damn well made it!

I'm filled with a familiar euphoria. I've conquered the odds before. Overcame adversity. Proven myself better than those humans I despise. I'm different to them. Better. A string of words enters my head: _Never mess with Vatic, or he'll fuck you over._ I play them over, repeatedly.

A boy stands above me. My rescuer. I say _boy_, he's in his early twenties. A healthy mix of races lends him soft, warm features. His attractive light-brown face is all wide eyes framed by big hair—long, blond curls spilling over his shoulders. His skinsuit is already loose around his ankles, naked apart from a pair of short briefs. He's not overly muscled but well-balanced. And he likes himself. That much is evident.

"Man, I thought you'd be dead for sure," he says. "You okay?" The panic and anger I sensed before has disappeared, to be replaced with pride at his achievement.

"Yeah, I just love dancing on the hangman's jib… Thanks for cutting me down."

"Er… what?"

I stare into him. I've no idea where the words came from, but they fit me like a glove. "Forget it. I only say thank you once." The sentence is coughed out as I start dry retching again.

His brown eyes widen. "I heard you guys were arrogant… guess they were on the money."

The inner airlock door opens to reveal a pile of clothes hurriedly left on the floor. Before I can ask him what he means, he strides over, his naked feet slapping the metallic decking. He dresses himself—keeping his eyes on me.

Finally, my wracking stops, which seems to encourage him to speak.

"You were in space for over ten minutes without oxygen and you're still breathing. That's kinda cool. You sure you're okay?"

I free my head from the tight-fitting hood and release my tangled mass of thick black hair.

"Man, you're a mess." He offers me a well-formed hand and pulls me to shaky feet.

I remember the image on the wafer. The mad, freaked out eyes. The hungry expression. "I suppose I am."

"And you're short."

He towers over me by a good foot. "Yeah, and I thought you'd be older. I take it you're not Director Frederix."

"I'm nothing like that stuffed shirt!" he scoffs. "I'm Bill Jarrad. An intern. Think of me as the general dogsbody. This is the Zeta-Karst Laboratories. One of the Company's many research bases—although this is the best, not that you'll believe me once you start meeting people. I'm chief cook, coffee maker and your welcome committee… you're lucky to be alive."

I shrug, knowing I'm different from him. From everybody. I search my psyche expecting to find a feeling akin to pride, but instead discover resentment and anger. "I'm Vatic."

He stares at me like I'm something special. "So are you gonna tell me or not?"

"About what?"

"The deal with your crazy spacewalk?"

I shrug again. "They wanted rid of me asap, and threw me out the airlock."

"It sure seemed like that."

I round on him. "There's no 'seemed' about it. I don't lie, okay? I never lie."

"Okay, calm down. If you say you were thrown out into space without oxygen, then I'm not going to disagree. And, by-the-way, I did rescue you. So you might want to go easy on me."

"I'll try my best."

"We only received a brief transmission. A ship in orbit saying they were leaving someone to pick up. I know you're Skilled, but I thought you'd be dead for sure. Who did this to you?"

"Some jerk from the Company. *Strategist Stranng.*"

"He sounds like an idiot."

"You don't know the half of it. I got the feeling Stranng didn't much care for this job." And in this moment, I decide to make that bastard pay—if I ever get the chance. I'm on the clock. Under six hours and counting, but as soon as I'm done…

"When I was told the Company was sending in a Skilled, well—"

"Well what?"

A frown creases Bill's smooth features, hanging peculiarly, like the expression hadn't yet learnt how to fit his face. "You're not what I was expecting."

"You're disappointed?"

The kid says nothing. He doesn't have to. I get it. The Company told him I was someone important, a top-notch investigator and here's this longhaired, emaciated madman with a bad attitude. "This isn't my best look, granted." I shrug. "And I'm not really sure what the hell I'm doing here, but this is what you've got. I suggest you try and live with it."

The frown appears again, this time more ingrained, and I sense sudden anger, although the grimace is not directed at me. Either way, psychoanalysing this kid will get me nowhere.

"Just answer me one thing," he says finally. "Are you the genuine article or not?"

"And what's the genuine article?"

"Someone to put the willies up Director Frederix and the rest of the creeps on this station. *The Skilled.*"

I take a deep breath and fix him squarely with my eyes. "Like I said, I'm Vatic. That's all you need to know."

He stares back at me for a few seconds before striding away. "Follow me."

We enter a functional chamber serving as the base Auxiliary Hub. The space is large enough to house other machinery and, compared to the spaceship I just vacated, this is pristine. Smooth white walls gleam under softened lighting. Well-kept service drones stand in long lines, lights flashing in the green. A further annex contains skinsuits, helmets and oxy-tanks hanging in ordered rows next to a bank of impressive lockers. A two-person bug is docked on one wall, and beyond, through low rectangular windows, I can see a landing pad at the end of a long raised service way. I'm impressed. The Company I half-remember was bureaucratic, slow-moving and always cutting corners. The Zeta-Karst Laboratories are on a completely different level. "So what goes on here?"

"Important research. Top Secret and all that hush-hush crap. You know the Company drill—I say one misplaced word and my career is over and done with. Deleted and thrown in the trashcan. But there's no chance of that. The guys here, the scientists, don't let anything slip. They're paranoid about their research, frightened it's going to get stolen. Other than their names and fields of study, I'm in the dark—and I prefer to keep it that way. Now let's get you something to wear." Bill opens a few of the lockers, the doors swinging with controlled hisses and clicks, and produces a 'boiler suit'—the colloquial name for any generic nano-wear. A white blank, fully adjustable to any number of style and colour requirements. "This'll probably fit you. Belonged to Irenka. She was about your size. She left just after I arrived." A wistful look passes across his face.

He had history with Irenka… or had missed his chance. "I prefer the skinsuit."

"You frightened of depressurisation, huh?"

"I'm not sure. Let's just say I like the look, okay?"

"There's no danger of a hull breach, not unless we're hit by something as big as the asteroid we're on. Which is pretty damn unlikely." He shakes his head, blond locks brushing against his shoulders, his eyes flicking around the superstructure. "This base has the best automatic recovery and sealant systems in the whole Company."

Pride radiates from Bill. I suppose being an intern at the Company's top lab must be quite something, even if he is a dogsbody. "Where are we going?"

"Habitation Section. Director Frederix is waiting for you. He's pretty peeved the Company sent in a Skilled. It's just a dumb suicide after all."

"You think the death was suicide?"

"Yeah, nasty."

I follow him out of the airlock. "So Bill, you gonna fill me in on what I'm supposed to be doing here?"

His head dips and his eyebrows raise. "Didn't they give you a brief?"

"As of forty minutes ago, I was in hypersleep. My

memory is all shot to pieces. First, tell me about the Skilled. Tell me what I am."

The kid stops for a second and I nearly walk into him. "You don't know?"

"The Medic said my memory will start coming back to me soon. In the meantime…" I indicate for him to continue.

Bill purses his lips and shrugs. "The Skilled was a sort of nickname for the Company's Special Police. Genetically engineered enforcers—illegal of course—but engineered all the same. Empaths who could read emotion and intent." He continued walking, with me at his side hobbling on stiff legs. "They were hard-wired into the now, into the moment—seeing things in people that others couldn't—with full control over their autonomic nervous systems. That's probably how you survived your little jaunt into space."

He's right. I remember closing down the pain from my chest and pushing blood to my vital organs. All done consciously. I also notice Bill is using the past tense. "All that changed?"

"The Wars."

I say nothing, but I'm aware of something black inside of me. Dark, and purposefully hiding.

"You don't remember? Jeez! You guys were heroes. You won the war for us. In some quarters, you and your kind are venerated."

"Strategist Stranng didn't seem to venerate me. Rather the opposite."

"Let's just say the Skilled were more than effective. After the Wars, everything changed. The Company saw them as a threat and tried… to discontinue them."

"A threat?"

"The Wars altered a lot of people. And the Skilled were no different. They returned obsessed with truth, with getting to the bottom of things. My guess is that they were lied to, or at least given misinformation by the Company. Something happened. I don't know what—some say a failed coup, others that the Company moved against them, tried to wipe them out—but suddenly, the Skilled vanished."

"Then what am I doing here?"

Bill raised slim shoulders and let them fall again. "The Company must've kept tags on you in case you were required. I guess you were… *required.*"

"For a simple suicide?"

"This is their top research lab. They probably wanted their best operative."

I sense even more pride in the kid. "And that's me, huh?"

The kid laughs. "I suppose you must be, despite appearances. We'll just have to trust that the Company knows what they're doing."

"That doesn't fill me with confidence."

Bill laughs again. "If poor Chen Jelinek didn't crush himself to death, I'd be surprised. Either way, it looks like you're the man who's going to find out."

I take in the name and enter it into memory. *Chen Jelinek.* The victim. "Crushed by what?"

"Hey, I'm not doing your job for you. Saving your life is my limit, okay?" he winked. "The Company brought you here for a reason. I ain't gonna tread on their toes. No way."

Despite the humour, Bill is nervous and expectant.

I sense heightened anxiety in the boy—and what the hell does that actually mean? That I really am an empath? The word resonates inside of me…

That's exactly what I am.

suicide

WE ARRIVE in Habitation a short while later—the massive central dome I'd seen from space. A circular communal area leading off to a canteen and a control room of sorts. The rest segmented into modular living areas and corridors. No different from other installations, except that in this place, no one has attempted to make it feel like a home. Bare, white-metalled walls remained bare. Despite its name, Habitation has an antiseptic vibe that I dislike immediately. Cold and without any emotion. Various in-built furniture—tables, chairs, sofas—are dotted here and there. They appear unused, their surfaces shiny and new.

A few alcoves reveal games nodules and other typical recreational niches, yet my mind is taken by the canteen. I guessed the Medic must've given me some energy shots, otherwise I wouldn't be able to function, but my gut requires solid food… and something to drink. And I don't mean a glass of water.

I take out my wafer and flick the screen into life. In the top left corner is a countdown:

5 hours, 17 minutes.

That's how long I've got to solve this thing. Five hours and seventeen minutes before my organs begin to fail.

A man in his late fifties, radiating authority, waits for us, the tips of his fingers pressed together in expectation. He wears a well-fitted jacket of yellow and cream, chino-like trousers and a thick, red, velvet tie. It's an old-fashioned look. Quaint almost. At the sight of me, he visibly baulks. I'm not what he was expecting, that much is obvious. Then again, I'm not looking my best.

"Good afternoon, I am Director Anton Frederix," he says unfazed. His hands part, offering a handshake. A gold ring on his pinkie. His nails well-tended. A showy golden chain hanging around his wrist. "I always like to press the flesh, so to speak. It helps me get the measure of the man."

I take his hand and shake. The man's palm is dry, slippery. "I'm Vatic."

"Is that what I call you? Just Vatic?" he says with an exaggerated drawl.

I nod.

"Well met… Vatic. Well met." Milky blue eyes sparkle at me from behind gold-rimmed glasses, although he's unable to hide the distaste that crosses his face. The man doesn't want me here. Other than that, I sense nothing. He possesses a full head of longish, dark-blond coiffured hair pushed behind his ears. The style is almost feminine—yet he radiates exaggerated masculinity. I'm in his territory and he wants me to know that. "I hope you had a pleasant journey?"

I push back my own ragged hair and give a quick shake of my head. "Let's say my trip was eventful and leave it there."

Bill guffaws.

Frederix glances at the kid. "The intern been treating you well?"

"Yes, he's—"

"Good, good. Now Bill, run along, will you."

The kid shrugs at me, his eyebrows rising to frame a hurried smile. "Laters." He spins on one heel and strides away.

Frederix sighs and shakes his head. "Sorry about him. He won't be staying at Zeta-Karst for much longer. He's incapable of tying his own shoelaces without falling over. The boy has got too much attitude and not enough up here." He taps his forehead. "Know what I mean?"

I don't answer.

"Come this way."

I follow him to a door marked 'Laboratories Director' and we go inside. His office is a total contrast to the Habitation area—busy with tables and bookcases, paintings and various sculptures. A vast plasti-desk, behind which are hung the typical credentials of Frederix's profession, dominates half the space. On top, sits his data-centre—with the privacy screen enabled. The other half of the office is part science library, part gallery. An ancient Newtonian telescope stands next to an overly ornate brass microscope and other scientific instruments I don't recognise. All are reproductions, fakes. A hand-cranked Orrery of the Jovian system has pride of place by a drinks cabinet. I notice bottles of various amber-coloured spirits and feel a stab of intense desire.

As well as being a shrine to the concept of the accomplished scientist, this office has another object of worship: Director Anton Frederix himself. Bronzes and photographs of the bespectacled man litter the room. A digivid of him fills an entire wall. The image is less portly than the original and overly grandiose. Frederix likes himself. That much is for sure.

The Director bustles forward and sinks into a plush leather-effect chair behind his desk, beckoning me to sit down opposite.

I ignore him and go over to the drinks cabinet. I pour myself a stiff shot of whisky. Down it and pour another. Only then do I sit, taking the quarter-full bottle with me. Unlike everything else in this office, the drink is authentic. I'm impressed. The whisky hits my stomach like a bullet.

"Good choice," says Frederix, nodding at my glass. "There's no such thing as a beer budget at Zeta-Karst. We want something… the Company provides. And I'm not ashamed to admit I possess Champagne tastes. That's one of my finest ryes—an eighteen-year-old single malt."

He's annoyed, despite his pretty words and I don't have time for pleasantries. "Why don't you explain to me why I'm here?"

The Director sits back in his chair. "Suicide. As far as anyone can tell. Cut and dried."

"Go on."

"I can trust you?"

I shrug and down the second shot as Frederix tries to hide a grimace. "The Company employs us both, Anton. Tell me everything you know."

"You were not briefed on what we do here?"

A quick shake of my head.

"Well let me say that the research we are doing is top secret. You get my drift?"

"That doesn't concern me." I fill the shot glass again and take a fresh gulp of whisky. "I live for truth. To get to the bottom of things. Think of me like a relentless assassin. I never give up until I get the guy. *And I always get the guy.*" Again, the words spill easily off my tongue. A rehearsed speech I've used many times before.

Frederix's eyes narrow behind his gold-rimmed glasses. "Quite…"

"Chen Jelinek, the dead man, was he working on anything contentious?"

"Nothing unethical. I suppose with his research now defunct and the man himself departed, I can… spill his particular bag of beans. Chen was an artificial gravity specialist. His area involved using focussed, local grav fields to create invisible walls—a sort of energy shield. A real money-spinner if he could have made it work yet—"

"He wasn't successful?"

Frederix's face attempts a look of sorrow. "There was a lot of expectation on him. Sadly, he bit off more than he could chew. I think he over-egged the project. Made energy shields sound more possible than they actually were."

"Maybe he had a breakthrough and someone stole

his invention? That would be a motive to bump him off and make murder look like suicide."

"Sure, that could be a reason, but he took the honourable way out as soon as he learnt the Company had ended his tenure."

I've heard of the term 'end of tenure' before. A Company euphemism for getting the sack. A handshake and damn little else. No cramped room in an over-crowded housing development. No pension. Nothing. "Bad news for Chen," I say, feeling genuinely sorry for the poor sap.

"The end of his career."

I take another chug of whisky. More than anything I want to let the rye slam into my system, to blur my returning memories. But I hold the booze back, allowing only a trickle to enter my bloodstream. Being Skilled certainly has benefits. "Wasn't he one of the Company's stars? He'd have to be, working in a place like this."

"That is the heart of it," Frederix continues, seemingly in love with the sound of his own voice. "Getting to this level is not like a commission or any regular job. The Company invests thousands of post-war dollars into their careers. You've seen this base? Seen how this installation is a cut above? Guessed at the serious amount of credits spent in its creation?"

He looks at me expectantly. My answer is a slurp of whisky.

"Zeta-Karst is a make or break laboratory, Vatic. Scientists either do or die here. Chen, unfortunately, failed the litmus test."

The Director's lazy drawl—his slow, pompous way

of speaking—coupled with a heavy reliance on cliché and idiom is starting to grate on me. "They could defect," I say, finding that I'm arguing just for the sake of it.

"Who would take a failed scientist? No one. Not even any of the Company's rivals. And besides, we're both more than aware of how the Company deals with traitors." He gives me a knowing look. "Now, if you consider the rewards," he continues as if talking to a child, "if they make a breakthrough, if they bring in a sizable profit? Then they're deemed well worth their salt and set up for life. It is simple Darwinism—the survival of the fittest."

I decide to cut through the crap. "When and how did Chen die?"

"This morning in his lab." Frederix steeples his fingers, a look of false sadness creasing his face with conscious exertion.

"Tell me what happened, step-by-step."

"As Director, I tried my best to help him, but the man was simply asleep on the stick. The Company expects results—there is no such thing as a free lunch. They pay—we provide. Simple mathematics. He was sitting where you are just hours ago when I informed him that, regrettably, the Company had pulled the plug. That his research and career were now nothing more than tatters and ruin."

"How did he take the news?"

"Surprisingly well. He'd been under pressure for many months. I got the sense that the millstone around his neck had been removed."

"And you?"

"What do you mean?"

"I mean; how did you feel about his death?"

"Of course, I was very upset to lose him."

Lie. And don't need any inbuilt empathy to tell me that. I sit forward and stare at the man. "How did you really feel about his death? And this time, cut the crap."

The false look of sadness disappears, replaced with something far more calculating. Frederix leans back in his plush chair, contemplates me for a few seconds, and then speaks. "I can see you are a man after my own heart, Vatic. Someone who likes to cut the crap. Am I right?"

I wave the question away with an irritated hand.

"I didn't like him," he continues, spitting out the words like poison. "To be honest, when I heard he was finished, I was more than relieved. He was an irritant. Not exactly a troublemaker, but he rubbed people the wrong way. So yes, I wanted the idiot out of my hair. I have a responsibility to make sure this base runs smoothly with as little drama as possible."

"Then Jelinek left your office and offed himself?"

"Yes. And good riddance is what I say. He went to his laboratory and did the deed soon afterwards."

"Security footage?"

A quick shake of his head, as if my question is irrelevant. "The security system has been kaput for a few months off and on. Even when it worked, the coverage was for access corridors and shared living areas only."

I can hardly believe it. "You're telling me everyone has carte blanche to wander around the base with no monitoring system?"

The Director shrugs and straightens the cuffs on his old-fashioned jacket, giving every impression my enquiry is inconsequential. "What of it? As long as the labs are secure, which they are, the Zeta-Karst monitoring system is of secondary importance."

"And you say it's been off and on… what do you mean by that?"

"It's to do with the way Chen Jelinek killed himself. He set the AG—the artificial gravity—in his lab to over one hundred and thirty Gees."

"And how does that affect the security footage?"

"It was not the first occasion this had happened. Every time he conducted one of his tests, the energy drain caused a massive outage in the base and, amongst other problems, knocked out the security set-up. Power goes to the essential systems only. Life-support, lighting and auto-repair, but when the full systems returned, the cameras didn't. I requested the Company send a maintenance crew, which they finally did—anything not vital to my scientists and their experiments, you understand, is low on the Company's agenda. They are birds in a gilded cage and treated that way. The system was fixed with no problems, but Chen did another of his damn tests and…"

"You decided not to bother the Company again."

The Director straightens his tie with a delicate motion of his fingers. "Why swim against the tide? At least I can now get a crew in knowing Chen won't be around to stuff everything up."

"And he used his artificial gravity generators to

kill himself?"

"Crushed to death by his own hand. Massive bodily trauma. I was surprised. I didn't think the man had it in him—but who knows what any of us will do when our balls are slammed against the wall? A quick way to go, if a little messy."

I take in the information quietly, filling my glass to the rim and dipping my tongue in and out of the whisky. The single malt stings deliciously. "Where's the body?"

"Still in his lab. Untouched. I locked the laboratory as soon as I saw what he'd done. I know the protocols." He pauses, readjusting his glasses on the bridge of his nose. "I certainly didn't expect a Skilled to be put on the case."

It's my turn to pause. I stare into his pale blue eyes, half-expecting to read the man but get nothing. "Did he leave a note?"

"Not that I'm aware of. I also sealed his rooms. He may have left something behind in there. We will only know for sure when we go inside." The Director gets up and strides over to his drinks cabinet. He pulls another bottle and pours himself a shot. "Down the hatch!" He takes a gulp, holding the whisky in his mouth for a second, and swallows. "Do you have any idea why they sent you?" he says with feigned nonchalance. "This is open and shut."

"You're that sure it's suicide?"

"Don't pretend you care what I think. You're convinced it's murder and are champing at the bit. Why else would the Company send you?"

I ignore the question. "Did you kill him?"

Frederix shakes his head vehemently.

I try to read him, try to use my empath abilities—whatever they are. I get nothing. All I feel is an intense dislike for the man. "Could someone else have done this to him?"

"There's only five possibilities. Bill, who you've already met, and four other scientists."

"I'll need to meet them."

"I've ordered everyone to make themselves present in Habitation at sixteen-hundred hours."

I glance at a clock hanging on the wall. An actual antique. A black cat printed on the dial. Its tail and paw pointing out the time. Cute. It says one-thirty in the afternoon. To me, it's still early morning. And from what I can tell of myself so far, I'm not a morning person. "Three hours? No way."

"I'm sorry–"

"It's simple. The Company didn't send me to Zeta-Karst to piss about. I'm gonna take a shower, get a shave and while I'm doing that I want a meal prepared. Get everyone to Habitation in half-an-hour for a meet and greet. I've got full access to every section and every room. Including the labs."

Frederix smiles at me. All tight-lips and insincerity. The kind of smile that deserves a good slap or three. "Vatic," he says casually. "I get it. Your job is to cowboy up, to act as the fast-talking hard guy. But Zeta-Karst is no seedy backwater. You can't come here chewing knives and spitting bullets and expect everyone to jump like they're nobodies. These are scientists at the top of their respective fields running experiments vital to the future of the Company. They won't stand for such behaviour. We have protocols and agreed ways of conduct. And besides, this is my operation. I've been here for years. I know the place and the people. I'll help you the best I can, but… you'll do what I say. Do we understand each other?"

I down the rest of the whisky in a single gulp and say nothing.

"I said, do we understand each—"

I throw my shot glass at the wall behind Frederix's head. The tumbler smashes, showering him in crystal shards. He jumps like a cat bitten by the mouse it was hunting.

"You heard my instructions," I say with as much quiet threat as I can muster. "Follow them or not. But be warned, I possess the full authority to arrest anyone who impedes my investigation. That includes you. *Do you understand?*"

Throwing the glass was instinctual. It happened before I realised what I was doing. I see it now. Clear as day. This is a power play. I'm establishing who is boss here. I have to if I'm going to survive. I have to treat everything as if I'm back out in space, asphyxiating. I have to do as much as I can, because if I don't, I'll be as dead as Strategist Strang wants me to be.

Frederix opens his mouth to speak.

I lift a finger and press it against my lips. Most of my memories are shot to pieces, yet I possess an intrinsic understanding of my role here. I've played this part before, even though I can't remember anything specific. "I'm working for the Company," I say. "On their orders. Which gives me all the authority I need. So I'll ask you again. Do you understand me?"

The Director sags, nodding

"I'm in charge here. You do what I tell you."

Frederix puts his whisky glass to his lips, nods again and knocks it back.

"Good, I'm gonna use your shower."

The Director doesn't move.

"Your shower? Where is it?"

"But there are many other—"

"Don't waste my time, Anton." This is another power play. First, remove the top dog, and then use his private pissing grounds.

Frederix slams his glass down and strides towards a door. We enter a small corridor and emerge into what must be his living quarters. Like Habitation, these rooms consist of a central hub-like recreational area from which I can plainly see bedroom and shower cubicles. This space is too neat for my liking. Ordered. Clean. I feel like I've entered a cheap yet well-run motel. "You sure these are your quarters? The place doesn't look lived in."

Frederix shrugs. His glare tells me everything I need to know. He's uneasy with me in here. I decide to play on that unease. I take a swig directly from the whisky bottle I'm still carrying and start opening and closing cupboards and drawers. Frederix does nothing, and I admire his calm.

A large, full-length mirror hangs on one of the walls. I catch a glimpse of myself and I'm not a pretty sight. A calorie-challenged lunatic complete with manic hair, beard and bottle of booze. The skinsuit gives me a desperate look—and that's what I am. Desperate to get to the bottom of whatever is going on here. Desperate to get off this rock and away from people. *And desperate to survive.*

I stroll over to the shower cubicle. "Any reason why you're still here?"

Frederix says nothing.

I chug down the remaining whisky and thrust the empty bottle at him. "Then get out."

grandees

THE SHOWER is intoxicating, yet I can't dwell too long. Despite the high setting, the almost scalding water can't touch the deep cold inhabiting my limbs. My marrow is frozen.

Afterwards, I root around in Anton's shower room cabinets and find a pair of scissors. I cut away my wet hair with practised ease. I've obviously done this before. I sweep the black mass back, leaving it thick and bushy, hanging just above my collar—if I had one. I trim as much off my beard as I can before going for the razor. I set the machine to my preferred grizzled, unshaven look. Like in the 3D portrait, Stranng showed me. I feel better already.

Still shivering, I emerge from the drier and pull myself back into my skinsuit. There's an intimacy to how the fabric fits my body. Intelligent nanofibres adjusting to my emaciated limbs. It's comfortable and more importantly, functional. I check my reflection again. The mad-haired lunatic has gone. In his place—just your regular whack-job. I have no memory of clothes, of 'my style', though I look the part. Whatever that means. For the first time since I woke up, I feel like me. Like Vatic.

I flick the wafer into life, my eye drawn to the countdown:

4 Hours, 47 minutes.

Time is slipping away. I swipe through a few screens until I find the base roster. Six names highlighted. Four men and two women. I navigate my way around the menus with practiced ease. I have full access to every laboratory, toilet or broom cupboard. Just like Stranng said.

I do a proper search of the Director's rooms. Last time was just for show. I examine wardrobes, drawers, closets for secret compartments and hidden doors. Everything in his cupboards is pristine. There are multiple versions of an identical yellow jacket, wrapped in plastic. The same for his shirts, trousers and ties. I rub the material between my fingers. Cotton, wool and silks. It seems Frederix has a penchant for old-fashioned clothing. This stuff is expensive and difficult to keep in good order. He even has a pile of archaic boxer shorts and—of all things—socks. You'd never catch me in such clothes—I much prefer my skinsuit, but I'm impressed. The antiquated weave feels like nothing I've touched before. I'm about to end my search when my eye is caught by modern clothing poking out from behind his rack of faux-leather shoes. Half-hidden. A closer inspection reveals it to be an undergarment of close-fitting, intelligent nanofibres. Not exactly sexy, yet intimate and female. Does the outfit belong to one of the two women on the base? It's a possibility I can't ignore.

I next check Frederix's dressing table. The piece of furniture is over-elaborate, like the man himself. Covered in brushes, combs and more gold-themed trashy jewellery. A locked box is thrust behind the mirror—not exactly hidden, just out of the way.

Out of sight out of mind.

A locked box is like a mystery in itself. The case is heavy and something rattles inside. No time for prosaics. I go back to the shower, retrieve the scissors and jimmy the lock. Inside—an old Company war medal. A gaudy thing, faux-gold with crimson inlay. I flip the badge over. The inscription on the back says 'Anton Frederix—For Bravery Above and Beyond.' From what I know of the man, he probably bought this decoration from some cheap memorabilia store, or had it specially commissioned. I hold the piece in my hand for a few moments, staring. Memories bubble under the surface of my mind, but nothing solid. I return the medal to its box, and place it back in its hiding place before returning to the Director's office.

I head straight over to Frederix's drinks cabinet…

Empty.

Frederix has second-guessed me. I decide to not make the same mistake again. Cursing, I open the door and enter the short corridor that takes me to Habitation.

Five people wait for me. Director Frederix and four others—two men and two women in heated discussion. A discussion that stops when they see me. Like children awaiting punishment. I feel a sudden revulsion. Not exactly hatred, more a deep-seated dislike of all humans. I don't fit in with them. I'm different. I don't share their petty concerns. And there's another thing… *they have never liked me.*

I walk straight past their silent faces—not even bothering to give them the once over—and enter a large kitchen dominated by a long plasti-table. Delicious smells of cooking waft from the stove. Bill is here, frying what looks like an omelette, his hair tied back. I'm almost drowning in my own saliva. He acknowledges my altered appearance with a wink and a mouthed 'cool'.

I lower myself onto a frail looking tin-like chair and wave for the others to come join me. Bill drops the plate on the table and, grabbing a fork, I start to eat my first meal in space knows how many years.

Frederix sits down in the chair next to mine. I feel his proximity keenly. The others join him. A quick glance reveals a set of annoyed and worried faces. Two women. A large man with piggy eyes and glasses too small for his face and a guy with long hair tied into a ponytail and wearing a skinsuit like mine.

"I'm Vatic," I announce. "The Company sent me." I hold up the wafer. "I'm patched in to the com system. You want me. You find me through this."

Bill spins the remaining chair around and sits down, leaning his elbows on the back rest. "You sure scrubbed up well."

I ignore him and toss the female undergarment onto the table. "Found in Anton's quarters. So which of you two ladies does this belong to?"

"You bastard!" shouts Frederix. "I lent you my room so you could get showered. I did not expect you to—"

"Can it!" I say, shovelling another forkful of omelette into my eager mouth.

Frederix's milky blue eyes glaze over with anger and I squeeze down a smile. The two women sitting at the table do not stir. One is black, well-curved and in her early thirties, with a strong hint of Asian around her abnormally large eyes. The other is white-skinned—and I mean pure white—it's very rare to see that colour any more. Her blond-hair is just turning to grey. She's petite. A thin stick of a woman of indiscriminate years. She could be anything between thirty and sixty. Age treatments these days are expensive, but they're good.

"No takers?" I say. "Yeah, I'm not sure I'd want to own up either. Just know this—none of your personal secrets are safe from me, so you'd do best to hold nothing back."

Both women seem equally appalled at the accusation of sleeping with Frederix. I file the information for later.

"Now let's start again. I get you're all pissed at me for dragging you from your valuable work," I say between mouthfuls, "but I'm on the clock. Nothing I can do about it. The sooner we sort this out, the better for everybody." I pause. My little speech hasn't gone down well. "Two questions. Who was the last to see Chen Jelinek alive and who found the body?"

The black girl answers. Her outsized, brown eyes framed by long lashes give her an exotic look, but she's a plain Jane. Her short, ginger-tinted hair has partly receded to reveal a large, smooth forehead. It furrows and unfurrows as she speaks. "I found him dead in his lab," she says, her voice practical and measured. "After what happened this morning, it was no surprise."

I tap the wafer into life: *Offia Okonjo. Molecular Biologist & DNA specialist. Age: thirty-six.* I wonder if she is the one sleeping with Frederix. "So you also think his death was suicide?"

Before she can answer, the big man speaks up. He's enormous. An ape seemingly wrapped in a skin too large for his body. He wears a lab coat, the buttons stretching over his barrel of a chest. A row of pens in his top pocket completes his 'I'm a serious scientist' look. He has a full head of thick, cropped greying hair perched atop an expressive face of Indian descent. Iron-grey eyes contemplate me with undisguised hatred from behind a pair of oblong-lenses—his glasses jammed into the bulbous flesh of his face. "It's bad enough that idiot loser killed himself," he whines with self-importance, his voice peculiarly reedy and high-pitched for a man of his bulk, "but I am far too busy to be drawn up into this nonsense. I'm doing vital work for the Company. Work that cannot be interrupted. I'm only here because Frederix asked me personally. And until you can prove to me that this investigation is vastly more important than my work, I'm having nothing to do with it… or you!" He hits the table with a fist like a side of ham, the sound startling everyone including myself—although I don't show it.

Despite my relaxed exterior my pulse accelerates. I calm myself, slowing my heart, and flick the wafer in my hand. The giant is *Frank Ackermann. Robotics. Age:*

sixty-one. Winner of some important prize or other. I don't care about prizes. Neither does his bulk or attitude intimidate me. I stab him in his fist with my fork—a quick, forceful in-and-out jab.

Ackermann yelps like a punished dog.

My heart is racing again. This time I let it thud in my ears. "You'll do what I tell you. You all will," I say with a false serenity that impresses even myself. "Like it or not, I'm here on the Company's orders with their complete authority. Isn't that right, Frederix?" I don't look at the Director—my stare is fixed on Ackermann.

From the corner of my eye, Frederix nods and turns away in disgust.

The large man grabs his injured hand in shock, his tremendous jaw dropping onto his chest.

I motion to Bill for another fork.

The kid stares at me for a moment, a mixture of alarm and admiration crossing his youthful features. "...Yeah, sure." he says.

I feel a surge of excitement from him. He's both pleased and impressed by my display. I suppose that, from his point of view, me treating these so-called grandees like the spoilt brats they have become, is a welcome change. I also have a new esteem for the kid. To wait hand-and-foot on such egos day-to-day must be a real pain in the ass.

The others appear alarmed. I guess they've not seen anything quite like the show I'm putting on. The blond can't help a smile, while Offia stares at me with an expression akin to shocked respect. The longhaired guy remains impassive.

I grab a fresh fork from Bill and brandish the

prongs at Ackermann like a street knife. "So I'll ask again, and this time, Frank," I say with calm threat, "I want you to answer me. Do you believe Chen killed himself?"

The overweight scientist points his iron-grey eyes in my direction. He says nothing for a long time, his body quivers in apoplectic rage. "How dare you!" he says finally, the words emerging as a series of strangled squeaks. "I'm Frank Ackermann… How dare you!"

I sit back in my chair and continue to eat my meal. "You either comply with my questioning or I lock you up."

"The Company won't stand for it!" Ackermann bleats. "I won't stand for it!"

Frederix turns back to the table and puts a hand on the big man's arm. "Just answer his damn questions. The sooner he's done and out of our hair, the better for everybody."

Ackermann shrugs him off with a flick of his shoulders, though I can see he's defeated. It's like I thought—the man is all wind. Offia passes him a napkin and he presses the paper-cloth against his bleeding hand.

"It's a simple question," I say. "And this is the third and final time I'm going to ask. Do you believe Chen killed himself?"

"The man was a loser!" Ackermann spits out the words, his bulging cheeks chewing with fury. "I guessed what he'd done as soon as the power went out."

"How come?"

"You don't induce that many Gees without a

significant energy drain. And what else would he be doing? He was washed up."

The smooth skin of Offia's forehead furrows again. "And it wasn't the first time the power has gone off after one of Chen's experiments. My day's work was ruined, so I was pretty unhappy. I waited until the emergency power kicked in and went to give him a piece of my mind. That's when—"

"When you found the body," I say simply. "And during the blackout, there was no gravity?"

"No *artificial gravity*," says the blond.

The name on the wafer informs me this is *Trinny Lunn. Nanobiologist. Age: seventy-three*. I stare past Frank Ackermann's enormous frame and re-examine her. She possesses a certain beauty. The fat has gone out of her face—taut skin stretched over her high-cheekbones and her eyes sunken. The woman must have seen a lot in her seventy or so years. She could even be an Earth original—but I doubt it. They wear their heritage with arrogance. Trinny Lunn contains a different kind of pride.

"Karst has its own gravity field," Lunn continues, her exact words emitted one-by-one from the upturned lips of a full mouth. She reminds me of a school teacher—the particular tone used to impart information while the mind is somewhere else. "A minor asteroid. One-eighth gee."

I size her up. She is a better fit for the underwear I found in Frederix's rooms, although my bet is still on Offia. Frederix is a narcissist—that much is certain. Would he be willing sleep with someone over seventy? I'm not convinced, regardless of age treatments. And besides, Trinny Lunn didn't seem like the kind of person to leave her underwear lying around with creeps. I turn to Offia. "Did you see anyone on the way to Chen Jelinek's laboratory?"

Offia shakes her domed head.

"Is it possible someone could have murdered Jelinek and returned to their lab undetected?"

"Everything is possible," says Trinny Lunn. "But Chen killed himself. Like Frank said. He was finished here."

"See!" Ackermann shouts, sucking at his injured hand.

I turn to the one person I've not yet spoken to. The wafer tells me he is *Hassan Elbaz. Hydroponics Development & Specialisms. Age: forty-one.*

He looks older. His skin is tired from exposure to UV, tanned and sunburnt. Long, brown, sun-yellowed hair is held back by a red band around his forehead. Unlike the others, he perches cross-legged on his chair.

"Anything you want to add, Elbaz?"

A brief holier-than-thou shake of his head. A parting down the middle of his scalp shows each individual follicle precisely arranged.

I sit back in my chair. Unless I agree with them all—that this was suicide—this won't be easy. But something tells me that verdict is not why I'm here. And I have to get to the bottom of this sooner rather than later. "Who was the last to see him?"

Elbaz raises his hand.

"I thought you didn't have anything to say?"

His answer is a nonchalant shrug. He wears a

customised skinsuit, his feet naked—soles blackened and calloused. His hands, held flat with the thumbs hidden, rest atop a taut stomach. There's something wound tight and slightly animal about Elbaz—a predator, tense and ready to strike. I see it in the clench of his jaw, and the whites of his fingertips. The others sit a little away from him, or he from them. A loner. Probably happier with his plants and nutrients than with people.

I lean forward and stare into his snakelike eyes. "Don't play games with me, Elbaz. You may think I'm out of condition, but I can still kick you to one end of this base and back again if the fancy takes me." The threat comes from nowhere, yet part of me wants Elbaz to resist. I'm a fighter, I realise. Angry and eager to let my inner Neanderthal free—a simple black and white creature unconcerned with the greys of the higher mind.

Elbaz stays absolutely still, his face remaining impassive. If he's worried about my threat, he doesn't show the emotion. "He came to my lab."

"What for?"

A shrug and a nod of his head. "To talk, I guess. My domes are next to his. My labs are not off-limits, not like the others—I give people access if they don't disturb my work." He glared at Ackermann who scowled back at him. "He often liked to visit and, as long as he left me alone, I didn't mind."

"What did he say?"

Elbaz grabbed at the skin under his jaw with a tanned hand and squeezed. "He just asked how things were going. Smalltalk. I told him to come in and chill out—he'd had a shock. But he said he was busy."

"Busy? The man had just been sacked. Didn't you think that was odd?"

"Everything about Jelinek was odd. He was stressed, irritable and always sweating. Out of everyone, he seemed to like me. I don't know why. I never went out of my way to be friendly."

"Did he look worried?"

"I didn't meet him face-to face. I was working in one of my domes. We chatted over the com."

"So you weren't the last one to see him alive?"

Another shrug. "A few minutes after I closed the com—the time it took him to return to his lab and kill himself, I guess—the power went out."

"And the outage, did that affect you or your work?"

"If the gravity was off for more than an hour or two, then maybe. But it was an inconvenience rather than a problem for me."

Frank Ackermann threw up his hands in disgust. "This is nonsense. A total waste of time. Why would any of us kill Chen when we all knew he was leaving? Company excommunication is a fate worse than death. This whole thing makes no sense. And besides, not one of us would risk our own livelihoods and research. You're way off the mark, Vatic. Way off. And don't think I'm going to forget this. The Company will hear how you treated me today and it won't go good for you."

"And what exactly do you do, Frank?" I ask, rounding on Ackermann again. "Robotics is nothing new. What's your research?"

Ackermann's eyes flick towards my fork and he

pulls his hands away sharply. "Frederix, tell him the unwritten rule."

The fire seems to have gone from the Director. "We do not talk about each other's research," he says, his voice quieter than I've heard it before. "There's no bones about it. A simple base rule."

"We?" I'm intrigued. "Are you also doing experiments?"

Frederix nods to the wafer.

A quick tap. *Anton Frederix. Zeta-Karst Laboratories Director. Specialisation: Exo-Biological Research. Age: fifty-eight.* "Exo-biology? That's aliens isn't it?"

"I'm not at liberty to talk in present company, although I'm more than happy to discuss my work with you in private," he says through clenched teeth. He turns towards Ackermann. "As any of us would be."

Ackermann is not well-pleased with this answer. His piggy eyes glare at the Director like he's been betrayed.

I push my plate away, the omelette half-finished— my stomach must have shrunk to the size of a walnut. Or I filled myself up with whisky.

I thank Bill and stand up, my legs creaking. "Right, I'm done with you," I say with a dismissive wave of my hand. "I get you want to keep your work secret, so I'll be talking to you individually later on. I expect full disclosure. Now go back to your labs."

Everyone stands up. Ackermann pushes his chair over with a clatter and bustles away, cursing to himself.

"Offia?" I say, placing a restraining hand on her shoulder.

She spins quickly, shrugging me aside. The motion is feline and practised. I sense she is able to handle herself in a fight, should the need arise. Her eyes stare into mine, long attractive eyelashes batting in time to the furrowing of her high forehead.

"You're up first," I say, unfazed. Or at least pretending to be. "Take me to see the body."

Frederix falls in behind us. "Where are you going?" I ask without breaking my step.

"With you."

"No way! You stay here and help Bill wash up."

4 HOURS, *11 minutes.*

That's how long the wafer says I've got left. Time is slipping away and fast.

A quick look at the floor plans of the base shows me Habitation is a central hub surrounded by five labs all linked with short corridors creating a pentagon-shaped outer walkway around the perimeter. There are six exits, five leading directly to each respective laboratory or research dome. One extra hatchway—the one used by Bill and me to gain access to the base—links to the airlock chambers and the Auxiliary Hub a suitable distance away from the main complex. I also see what must be Elbaz's area—another base-sized installation of multiple domes. That's quite some hydroponics experiment.

Offia opens one of the hydraulically sealed hatches and we exit Habitation. She wears a green suit—trousers and jacket, both with various pockets and zips. The trousers fit tightly around her ass, which is not unpleasing. But there's a stiffness to her, as if she knows she's being watched—and not just by me.

I walk deliberately slowly, saying nothing, hoping the silent treatment will get her talking. She stays tight-lipped, her arms firmly crossed over her bosom.

The door closes behind us with a hiss.

The corridor, if it can be called that—an oblong no longer than twenty feet in length and wide enough for two people to walk abreast—ends in a hub-like crossroads of sorts. Facing us on the far wall is an alcove holding an impressive door, larger than the hatch we have just come through. Strengthened. *Chen Jelinek's laboratory.*

I'm pretty sure this is unimportant to the investigation, yet something about the undergarment I found in Frederix's quarters niggles me. Or maybe I'm a pervert. Either way I'm not yet ready to let it drop. I decide to lead from the front: "Are you Frederix's lover?"

Offia's brow furrows once, twice, three times, but she says nothing. I ask her the question again.

"No. I'm not his lover," she announces. "This girl's got taste."

"You think his sweetheart is maybe Trinny Lunn?"

"If you want to talk, let's do so away from prying eyes, okay?" Her gaze flicks upwards.

"The Director tells me the security system is off-line and has been for months. So what you worried about?"

"Oh I don't know… maybe that he's lying?" She charges off towards the closed hatch of Chen's laboratory.

I speed up and stop her with a hand around her arm. "You don't like the Director?"

"Let's get inside. I'll answer your dumb questions then, okay?"

We enter the dimly lit alcove. I take out the wafer and navigate to Chen Jelinek's lab. 'EYE SCAN REQUIRED' flashes at me. Retina-print technology is old and well-tested. With biometric signatures and detection widely used by the Company, this is a somewhat archaic addition to the security protocols. I put my eye in front of the scanner and, after a quick vertical up-and-down sweep, the hatch to Chen's lab opens with a series of clicks and whirs. I can see Offia is impressed. "Are all doors on this base protected the same way?"

Offia nods. "It's more than just an eye scan, there's a whole raft of security extras."

"Like what?"

"I dunno. They don't tell us that stuff."

I drag her inside, closing the hatch behind us. We're standing in another small, darkly lit access corridor.

"Thank space for that," Offia says, framed by the bright, white light coming from a large chamber beyond. Her whole body relaxes, her weight shifts from her upper spine down to her hips, her head thrown to one side. Suddenly, she projects attitude. "You can let go now, okay?"

I release my grip and Offia turns to face me. "You gotta know Frederix is listening to you. Watching everything you do."

"Maybe."

"There's no maybe about it. He's a control freak. He's always digging—attempting to figure out what everyone's up to. Trying to rip off our research."

"You really believe that?"

"Don't you understand? This is the Company's top science installation. Any info or tek Frederix steals from us he can sell for thousands of credits and a position in a rival company."

I flick my eyes at her. "Is that what you'd do?"

Offia holds my gaze. "You're the empath, you tell me."

"The Director doesn't worry me."

"He should do." Offia takes out a box of cigarettes from one of her many pockets and lights up. "You smoke?"

I nod before I realise my answer is yes. And with the realisation comes a deep desire. "I could murder one."

"Here."

She touches her cigarette to the end of mine, our faces in close proximity, and I almost lose myself in her abnormally large eyes. She pulls back, a wry smile appearing on her lips that I now notice are coated in a ruby lipstick.

Away from the others and the cameras she's convinced are following her every move, she's a different person. More confident, centred and… earthy. Maybe she's not such a plain Jane after all. There's a certain symmetry to her limbs, a pleasing curve.

I suck deep on the smoking tube of tobacco and cough like cancer. By the time I take my second and third drag, the coughing stops.

"That's how you do it, Cowboy," Offia says between

laughs. "All or nothing. But that's you all over… well, your type."

"You've heard of what I am?"

"The Skilled? You're kinda like heroes." She leans forward and kisses me on the cheek.

I'm unprepared for the sudden intimacy.

"And everyone likes a hero," she continues.

The warmth of her fleshy lips cascades out across my face and, before I realise it, I'm blushing.

Her brown eyes narrow. "You didn't strike me as the shy type."

I shrug. "I'm having an off day."

"You must be."

Is she making a play, trying to distract me? I admit it, I find her attractive. The way she changed, chameleon-like, after we entered Chen's lab intrigues and impresses me. I suck in another mouthful of cigarette, determined not to lose focus. "So as soon as the power and gravity returned, you came straight here, right?"

"We're back to that are we? And what kind of name is Vatic?"

"Just answer the question."

A look of resignation passes over Offia's face. "I was running an important multi-gene-sequence. The power outage ruined everything. A whole week gone up in smoke. It wasn't the first time Jelinek had been responsible for destroying my work. And I'm behind schedule as it is."

"Were you aware Chen had been given the heave-ho?"

"Yeah. I thought he'd shut the base down out

of spite." Smoke curls around Offia's fingers and crawls up towards her face. Her eyes sparkle in the dimness of the corridor. "We were called together for a meeting in Habitation last night. And Frederix told us the good news."

"Hardly professional."

"The Director is in charge here. It was his call. And he hated Chen as much as everyone else."

"And after Chen offed himself and the power returned, you came directly to Chen's lab. How did you get in?"

"The hatch was open."

"You think he left it that way deliberately, to be discovered?"

"Makes sense to me." She turns and strolls out of the connecting corridor and steps into the laboratory, one hand on her hip, the other sweeping her cigarette in front of her like a radar device.

I take in Chen's workshop for the first time. A warehouse-sized hemisphere full of improbable machines of vast dimensions. A cityscape of towering skyscrapers standing shoulder to shoulder in crazed proximity. Despite the size of this space, it's crammed almost to bursting with apparatus of all type and sizes—like the discarded experiments of some mad scientist hoarder. Wires and cables stretch between these mammoth blocks. Net-like arrays of glistening, silver mesh are suspended above like a spider's web.

I'm no claustrophobe, but the effect is suffocating. The dome is also as cold as a grave. "Did someone turn down the thermostat?" I ask, pulling my arms around myself and shivering.

"It's slightly chillier than outside, as there's a lot of hot tek in here needing a serious amount of cooling, although it's not that cold… You fresh out of hypersleep?"

"How'd you guess?"

"Hey, I'm a biologist, or doesn't your Company wafer tell you anything important? People can feel a deep sense of cold for up to six months after a long stint in hibernation. Turns out it's nothing physical, the coldness is all in the mind." She taps at her own extensive dome and raises her eyebrows as if I'm not quite there.

A splash of red amongst the silver and greys of the overcrowded equipment and I'm drawn to what must be the body—Chen Jelinek—half slumped over the remains of a collapsed horseshoe desk, half-pooled in a large puddle of still wet viscera and blood. "Is this how you found him?"

Offia's eyes flick over the mutilated half-corpse, before turning away. "Hu-huh."

I go over to the body—what's left of it—the floor is depressed in a perfect circle, everything inside, crushed, flattened and destroyed. Chen's desk is nothing more than so much compressed plastic. I can also just make out what is left of his data-centre. Also destroyed. Only Chen's legs remain, severed above the knees. "This is what one hundred and thirty gees looks like huh?"

"I guess so."

"Nasty." I examine the obliterated remains further. Nothing is recognizable. Not even bone. "Is this how you found him? Some kind of human pond?"

"You sure have a nice turn of phrase."

"I do my best. Now, answer the question."

"Nothing has changed."

"Take a proper look."

Offia turns and lets her brown eyes play over the grisly scene. "Yeah, that's how I found the poor sap."

"For a biologist, you seem a little squeamish."

"No one likes to be reminded of death."

"You seen a lot of it?"

"My fair share. Enough to not want to see any more… unless it's necessary."

I'm not sure why, but her sentence throws me.

Offia takes a long drag on her cigarette and blows the smoke out of her nose. "You feeling okay? You look kinda weird. Well… more weird than I expected for a Skilled."

"Define 'okay' and I'll attempt an answer."

She smiles. And yeah, she's suddenly pretty. One of those faces that only make sense when they come alive. Our eyes linger on one another a second longer than is comfortable—for me anyway—and I look away. "Let's get back to the investigation."

"Do we have to?" she says. "I didn't like Chen, but to die as he did. On his own. It's not the way Offia would want to go, that's for sure."

"It seems the perfect method to me. Very quick. If his death *was* suicide."

Offia bats her long eyelashes and nods solemnly. "It was suicide. Had to be."

A sudden thought hits me. "Why is there no Medic on the base? Every ship, space station or installation, has to have a medical officer. Company protocol."

"Not on Karst. Not since I've been here anyway."

"What about situations such as this? Sure, it looks like Chen was crushed to death. But how do we prove that? He could've been poisoned and then crushed. Or had his brains bashed in beforehand. The body might not even be Chen's."

"Making sure there's a Medic on base is the Director's responsibility, not mine. Why don't you go and ask him?"

"You trying to get rid of me?"

"Yes," she says unabashed. "You're more fun than I expected, but this girl is busy. And you are turning into a distraction."

Offia bats her eyelids again. She's quite the flirt, but is she sincere or not? I'm supposed to have a special ability for reading people—at least that's what Bill told me—but my empathy doesn't seem to be working. I must be off my game. I blame my inability on the hypersleep and memory loss, and let it pass. Besides, I don't have the time or the energy for any extra-curricular activity. "Did you find a note? Anything from Chen?" I say, ignoring her fluttering eyelashes.

If Offia is disappointed, she doesn't show it. She shakes her head.

I crouch down and take a closer look at the wrecked desk, accidentally dropping my cigarette into what was left of Chen. The smoking stub extinguishes in the puddle of gore with a loud hiss. "Chen's personal data-centre is most likely irrecoverable, but there has to be hard information storage for a project this size. I'm guessing he's using some serious computing power."

"Not anymore."

"You know what I mean."

"I'm no expert with computers, no more than any other scientist at the top of her field," she says with a side of sarcasm. "But Chen could've saved and protected his research in any number of ways. Everyone is worried about espionage, which must lead to many creative and covert data storage techniques."

Her answer sounds both truthful and convenient. I struggle back to my feet, my legs creaking with the effort. "Who is the top computer person on this base?"

"Before I met Trinny Lunn, I would've said 'me'. But she's some kind of computing savant."

"You ready to talk about her? You seemed a little tight-lipped in the corridor."

"The undergarment you found can't be hers. She despises Frederix. We all do. I may dislike the stuck-up bitch, but she's got too much self-respect and besides, she gets her kicks elsewhere."

"Elsewhere?"

"I'll come to that in a minute…"

"You know stuff?"

"Just the dirt."

"Well carry on then."

"When the Company sent me to Zeta-Karst Laboratories, I knew I'd be working on my own. That's the rule for everyone. We get access to the Company's tek, to its vast resources and unlimited credits, but actual human support is disallowed. Too much risk of espionage you see? When I arrived, Frederix had already been Director for quite a few years. I think the loneliness had gotten to him."

"He made a pass at you?"

"If you can call it that. He was as subtle as a meteor strike. Made a big show about wanting to get to know the real me. This girl's no prude, but some men are just—" She took a down a lungful of smoke and blew it angrily from her nose. "He may have made a similar pass at Trinny—but I can't see her responding… can you?"

"So where did that undergarment come from?"

"We all have secret lives. I have no idea what Frederix gets up to on his own time or when he's off-base." Offia's lip curled in disgust.

"He's often away?"

"Only as often as he's allowed. Everyone needs… *recreation*."

"So the clothing could have come from outside?"

"Just a guess. There's no shame in us using the, ahem, *Company operatives* from time to time, even if you are the creepy Director. He might have persuaded them to part with their knickers on a more permanent basis—if that's what he's into."

"Have you used the same service?"

"I don't have to. I have my own underwear."

"You know what I mean."

"Is this question really pertinent to your investigation?"

"Just answer me."

Offia pauses, takes a final drag of her cigarette and drops the lipstick-coloured stub on the floor, crushing it under the sole of her foot. "Like I said, the Company rule is we work alone. Sure, I've employed their talents—I'm a biologist. I, more than most, know how important a good dicking is to a healthy body and mind. Never here on the base, though. That's restricted."

"What about Bill?"

"I'm afraid he's taken."

"He is?"

"Yeah, the dirt I mentioned. Trinny made her move as soon as he arrived. They tried to hide their relationship, yet I knew what was going on. I'm not exactly a behavioural scientist, but I've always watched people. I like to size them up and fathom them out. She thinks him special, that much I do know. I catch her looking at him sometimes. I have to admit, I was surprised. I didn't think anyone could get to her. I left it a few weeks, hoping Bill might become bored, and change his emphasis so to speak. He wasn't interested. Maybe uptight white bitches are his thing."

"You like him?"

"Bill is a good kid. I say 'kid'—cos that's what he is. An intern. He reminds me of myself at his age. Naïve, eager to please, doing the shit jobs we have to do at the beginning of our careers in order to advance. And yeah, I suppose I shouldn't have hit on him. Days are long here and decent recreation… non-existent." She raises her eyebrows at me, her eyes glittering suggestively.

I find myself warming to Offia, even if she is deliberately trying to distract me.

"Frederix also had the same idea," she continues.

"He tried it on with Bill?"

She chuckled—a rich sound reverberating from

somewhere deep in her chest. "Poor Bill, he's been fighting us off left, right and centre. At least I was subtle. Frederix tried the whole 'I can end your career' thing on him. Credit to the kid—he told Anton to go stick it. Frederix is removing him next rotation."

"The Director certainly struck me as the vindictive type. What will Bill do next?"

"I dunno. He seems like a survivor."

I turn my attention back to the investigation. "Do you think Trinny Lunn will help us out here, with Chen's computers?"

An emphatic shake of her head. "You'll get no assistance from any of us."

Up to now, Offia has been mostly supportive and more than a little flirty. I'm surprised. "What does that mean?"

"It means no one on this base cares one jot about Chen dying. And if Chen Jelinek was murdered, I can't see the murderer helping with your investigation either, can you? And don't forget, we're busy people."

"Well it seems you've already forgotten who I am and my authority. As of now, I'm deputising you as base Medic. Okay?"

"I'm sorry, Vatic, but no way. I'm not getting involved. This girl is just too busy."

"Do I have to repeat the whole 'I can shut you down' speech? Cos I will, if you really need to listen to it again."

"And I thought I liked you."

"You're the closest to a Medic we've got. Probably better."

Offia takes out another cigarette, lights it and

makes a show of not offering me one. "You're not making any friends here, you realise that, don't you?" She blows smoke in my face.

"Get some samples from flat-boy over there. Check for anything out-of-the-ordinary. Toxins. Drugs. You know the drill. Do your best to determine what killed him—if it is actually Chen. How long will it take you to get some results?"

Offia shrugs. "An hour or two."

"No quicker?"

"I'll do the tests as quick as possible. I might even throw in a bar of candy if you say please."

"Good. The sooner I get to the bottom of this, the better."

"What's a matter Vatic? Don't you like free candy?"

"Offia," I say as nicely as I can muster. "Drop the act. You're getting tiresome."

"You think this is an act?"

"It doesn't matter either way."

"Not even a little bit?"

"I don't have the time to find out."

Offia's forehead furrows, and she sticks her bottom lip out in mock petulance. "You're a dick, Vatic, you know that?"

"Just focus on the tests. And watch yourself."

"You really think there's a killer out there?"

"I can't imagine the Company would've sent me here for a simple suicide, can you?"

Offia considers my words for a moment. "Knowing the Skilled, knowing how they *always get their guy*, if there is a murderer, wouldn't you be high on their kill-list?"

I round on her, putting my face close to hers. Staring once again into her big, brown eyes, I find an emptiness I'd not observed before.

"What is it?" she says, suddenly taken aback. "What do you see?"

"Did you kill Chen Jelinek?"

The eye contact doesn't break. "No, no I didn't."

domes

WE EXIT the outer hatchway of Chen's lab and step into the claustrophobic box-like hub. I nod my goodbye to Offia. Outside, back in the Zeta-Karst corridors, she's a different person. I sense she can look after herself, yet she's uncomfortable when out in the open—not that the passageways are anything but cramped. Her actions are akin to prey in a predator's territory. As to why she should feel like this? I have no idea. Unless she knows there's a killer on the base. Still, she was adamant Chen committed suicide. The change is something else, something that goes deeper into her psyche.

Offia is an unexpected distraction. Instead, I must focus all my efforts on the investigation. I glance at the wafer:

3 hours, 49 minutes.

I scroll through to the hydroponics expert: *Hassan Elbaz.*

Elbaz was the last person to see Chen alive—maybe he'll have some answers. I'm pretty sure he wasn't telling me the truth back in the canteen. Or at least, only half the truth. Hopefully I can read him better than I could Offia. His labs are the next to Chen's. I make my way down another modular corridor section—this one curved—and into another hub. Outside this hatch is a series of exotic looking plants sitting in a transparent shelf-like platform through which nutrients flow in clear, water-like liquids. The name display is greyed out—by fault or design. Either way, I know to whom these labs belong to. I hit the chime. A crackle followed by a voice. "Come in, Vatic."

The hatchway opens with clicks, whirs and metallic sounding thumps. I've never had much interest in hydroponics. They are cramped places—small bays stuffed with bright light, intense heat and the stench of rotting food and other biodegradable matter.

Instead of stifling warmth, I'm met by a long corridor full of cool air. I walk down the darkened tunnel, the temperature dropping with every footstep, until, a few minutes later, I'm shivering in front of another hatchway hung with thick, plastic transparent curtains from behind which glows what I guess is a UV source. I push through, hit by a strong smell of pine and a blast of freezing air.

I'm staring at a forest. Vast trees, over fifty feet high, tower over me. A coniferous woodland stretching far into the distance. Imposing and unexpected. I stumble backwards through the plastic curtains and back into the corridor, breathing heavily. I've never seen anything like it—not in the real. Sure, I've watched datavids and 'enjoyed the outside' with artificial reality, but to be in an actual forest, in person—it's a totally different experience.

I take a calming breath and push back through into the dome.

Everything is bathed in UV light, lending the green canopies a bluish tinge. The tree trunks are massive and intractable, but when I stare upwards, they appear impossibly high, like they might topple over at any moment. I'm dizzied and have to look at my feet to steady myself. Yet it's more than sight alone. My nose is overwhelmed by a cacophony of odours. The atmosphere is different, heady almost, and intoxicating.

This is nothing like the cold, anodyne corridors of ships and bases I've lived in all my life. Here are organisms growing, living, reproducing… *And I don't like it.* I'm used to straight lines, to order and regularity. The trees are like an insult to that.

I amble up to the first tree, ignoring the icy cold and kick aside the ferns brushing at my legs and feet. I run my fingers over the rough trunk. The bark is sticky. I notice an insect trapped in a thick, oozing liquid and tiny mites living in the wood. I'm disgusted. I guess the whole dome is also infested with the same creatures. It feels perverse, wrong and I'm glad I'm wearing my tight skinsuit.

"Don't forget your protection." Elbaz's voice over the com.

I go back to the hatchway and locate a series of visors hung on the wall. I put one on. The Plexiglas is clear, and cuts out the UV—draining the colour from everything.

"When you're done, make your way across to the central dome… I'm waiting for you."

I gingerly walk through the closely planted forest, the result of an ordered, yet creative mind. I see marks of pruning and husbandry—bonsai trees on a massive scale. The place is still outlandish to my senses. Inhuman almost.

The closest I've heard of anything like this is back on Earth, in the museums and preserves. No one other than dignitaries are allowed inside. If I ever get the chance to visit in the future, I'll give them a miss.

I delve deeper into the forest. Light is sparse under the thick, blue-green canopy and the silence eerie. It seems incredible that something so alive could be so still. The condensed foliage deadens my footsteps. Even the sound of my breathing—each gasp escaping from my mouth as a cold fog of chilled air—is like an intrusion. I follow a ragged footpath of sorts, made from collapsed boughs worn smooth by the regular passing of what I'm guessing are Elbaz's naked feet. And, suddenly, I'm consumed by irrational fears. That this is a maze of some kind, a trap. That I'll be wandering lost amongst these cold, freezing trees forever. A snap behind me and I whirl around, my heart racing. It's nothing, just a falling pinecone. My fears are illogical, born from this singular and bizarre experience. I slow my heartbeat and quicken my steps.

About halfway in, I get a funny feeling. I can't say any more than that. Just... *a funny feeling*. The trees here are sparser, and through them, I can spot an open space.

I leave the track, my eyes darting around, searching for—space knows what?—and tramp towards the clearing. The going is difficult, yet I'm rewarded by entering a wide glade. I say 'rewarded' though that isn't the right word. The area is full of dreadful black flowers. Fleshy, ebony-robed figures hanging from thin stalks—like hundreds of mini-gallows. I shiver, suddenly aware that the blooms surround me. The air has a strange aroma, heady and smelling faintly of decomposition and death. I turn quickly and retrace my steps.

With a certain amount of relief and self-reproach, I see again the outer wall of the dome and arrive at another set of plastic curtains. I push through into a second tunnel at the end of which are more curtains. I wonder what is waiting for me behind them. The atmosphere is thankfully warmer, although I'm still shivering.

"Vatic, you here yet?" Elbaz's annoyed voice, hissing over the com of the visor.

"Yes, just arriving in the central dome now."

"You okay?"

"Yeah, sure," I reply a little too quickly.

"You sound nervous. Make your way to the lake."

"Lake?" I blurt, unable to stop the word escaping from my mouth.

"I'm waiting for you there."

I take a calming breath and enter Elbaz's central dome. A blast of hot air and bright UV light and I find myself standing on the edge of a meadow. Again, I'm seeing with my own eyes what I've only ever experienced through a digivid. I'm in a vast, well-tended park—woods, grass, flowers and running water. The trees and plants are strictly ordered and trimmed—manicured. Bushes of all types and sizes are moulded and surreal looking. It's an improvement on the imposing forest I've just traversed, although the place still doesn't smell right.

I pad along a winding path made of well-fitted paving stones until I arrive in an awe-inspiring glade surrounding a sizeable lake. A wooden cabin, complete with porch, chairs and a small garden within which a series of vegetables are growing in tended lines, perches on the lake's edge. I realise a lot of work has gone into this simple vista: the lake, trees and cabin. Sitting on one of the chairs is Hassan Elbaz. He's wearing his tight-fitting skinsuit, a mixture of grey and scarlet. Upon his muscular frame, the outfit looks comfortable and well-lived in—a relaxed superhero ready to tackle any gardening or plant-related emergency.

He beckons me over with a supple sweep of his hand, his face deadpan, his cheeks lined and tired looking. Steely black eyes behind his Plexiglas visor stare at me with an edginess in contrast to his relaxed demeanour. He's trying to control himself, but I can tell he's nervous about this meeting. He wears no obvious weapons, although the man is wound tight—like a cobra ready to strike. I remember threatening him back in the canteen. I'll need to be careful.

I amble over, sitting down in the seat next to his.

Elbaz takes out a small pouch of tobacco and rolls a cigarette in his brown fingers. "None of the Company crap," he says. "This is all home-grown and sun dried. You want one?"

I'm not sure what he means by 'sun-dried'. The closest thing he has to sunlight are his UV emitters, but I nod. "You're not trying to poison me, are you?" I joke.

Elbaz shrugs, a quizzical expression appearing upon his face. "Not yet." He passes me the rollup and ignites the twisted end with a small electric lighter.

I put the homemade cigarette to my lips and inhale, realising just how much I needed another smoke. I tell my throat to ignore the hot vapours while simultaneously relaxing the bronchioles in my lungs. The nicotine infuses into my bloodstream without complaint, blurring my senses in a most agreeable way.

"Good?"

"Yeah," I say finally. "Very smooth." The tobacco is a cut above what Offia offered me and full of flavour.

A long pause as we enjoy our smokes.

"You don't like me," Elbaz says, a lack of inflection to his voice.

I ponder his words for a few seconds and answer. "To be honest, I don't like anyone that much. I'm here for an investigation, not a popularity contest. However, your work is ...*impressive*." I try my best not to grimace.

"I have six projects in total," he says with no emotion. "Jungle, desert, swampland and deciduous. You've seen the evergreen area and this is what I call my garden."

I take out my wafer and flick through the menu. I punch up the schematics for the hydroponics expert's lab. Six domes ballooning off the side of the base like cancerous growths. We are sitting in a central area from which, I guess, are four other hatchways leading to the hydroponic areas I've not yet seen. I think back to the closely packed trees and shiver involuntarily. "It must've been quite an undertaking to create that forest. I'm guessing years, right?"

"Five years, four months and seventeen days to be exact." The words hiss from his lips as if he's telling me how long he's been in prison, not working in this peculiar environment. The fact he knows the actual number is indicative of the man himself.

"My research is in accelerated growth via enhanced nutrients, energy and light delivery," he continues, with no sense of pride. Instead, his words contain an irate edge. "The evergreen dome you just walked through, if cultivated back on Earth, back before we built over everything, would've taken over twenty years to grow. From my point of view, five years is still a hell of a long time."

"If you don't mind me saying—isn't impatience a hindrance in this job?"

He turns his lined face towards me, eyes sparkling behind his UV visor. "And what do you know about my patience?"

I've touched a nerve—that much is for sure. "Look Hassan," I say, trying to connect with the man. "You have me at a disadvantage. I honestly knew nothing about you, your work or these domes before I arrived on the base a couple of hours ago. Why are you so eaten up?"

He sucks on his cigarette and blows the smoke out as one long breath. "I'm just surprised to still be here, that's all."

"What does that mean?"

"You work for the Company. You tell me." His voice is sharp with restrained anger.

"I'm at Zeta-Karst for one reason and one reason alone and that's Chen Jelinek," I say. "I know bugger all about the politics of this place. This is an investigation—a fact-finding mission, nothing more, nothing less. I'll ask you again and this time you can drop the attitude and give me some answers—why are you so eaten up?"

Elbaz's eyes narrow behind his visor becoming two glittering slits. "You really don't know?"

I answer with an impatient shake of my head.

Despite Elbaz's calm exterior, he sags into his chair. Tense muscles relax. Air escapes from his lungs in a long, rasping sigh.

I'm not what he was expecting.

"I've worked years on this." He waves his rollup in a dismissive arc at the scene in front of us. "I found out a few months ago that my research has been sidelined. Surpassed."

"Someone somewhere has more and bigger domes than the ones you've created?"

He gives a laugh like a man standing in front of a firing squad—hollow and full of dark acceptance. "Actually, it's the opposite. I received a message from a colleague I trod on along the way informing me of a new strain of research. A game-changer."

"And that was...?"

Elbaz takes a final drag and flicks his cigarette into the lake. The small stub hisses and sinks. "Bacteria," he says finally.

"Come again?"

"Despite every single one of these complex chemical interactions," he begins, "the beauty, the trees, grasses and plants—the insects and animals surviving in perfectly balanced systems—hydroponics exist for just two reasons: breathable air and food for off-world. And guess what? It turns out bio-engineered bacteria can do pretty much the same thing at a fraction of the cost and space. And the bad news doesn't stop there. The technology is earmarked to replace a whole range of other systems. There'll soon be no need for hydroponics at all. Instead, self-sustaining eco-bacteria will filter the atmosphere and provide illumination, coating walls and other surfaces like a sickly rash. All this…" He waves a brown hand at the vista of his work and grimaces. "All this is over. Done with. No more."

I don't like the place, but I can't help feeling angry for Elbaz. "They can't just shut you down."

"As far as the Company is concerned, I'm a dead man. I'm another Chen—waiting for the axe to fall. Waiting for my tenure to end."

I digest his words for a few moments. No wonder the guy is tense. "How long have you known?"

"Almost six months. Yet here I still am. Maybe they like making me sweat."

"This colleague could have lied to you."

A quick shake of the head. "She was gloating. And besides, I did my own checking."

"Then your work should've been shut down a long time ago."

He gives me a 'no shit'. "I can only guess that I have a friend in the Company. Or they have forgotten about me. Not that you care either way."

"You don't know me, Elbaz. And don't try to pretend you do." I stub out the rollup on the wooden arm of my chair and flick the remains into his garden. If this annoys him, he doesn't show it. The man is controlled. A loner, running this vast hydroponics experiment, never knowing when his life, as it was now, would be over. "What did Chen say to you? Really?"

The change in tack seems to surprise him. "You want to know?"

"I told you, that's why I'm here."

Elbaz seems happy to talk about Jelinek—maybe it's a relief from his own problems. "It made no sense. I've let him into my domes before and he'd just potter around. Recently, he's been spending a lot of time in the desert zone. I don't know what he liked about the place. The dome is mostly barren other than a single oasis and a few of my specialised cacti. Maybe he enjoyed the heat? But this time, he stayed at the hatchway and repeated the same phrase over the com: 'I am Chen Jelinek'. Manic-like. As if he was pleading with me to help him. 'I am Chen Jelinek. I am Chen Jelinek'. But what could I have done? I told him to get lost and offed the comlink. The next thing I know—the poor sap is dead."

"Why didn't you say that back in the canteen?"

"When I found out the fool killed himself, I dunno—I felt guilty. And why would I share that with the others? I don't like them. They don't like me. They're all new-comers, full of their own importance and certainty. The last thing I want is to give them ammunition against me."

"So you've been on Karst longer than anyone else?"

"Yeah, five years, four months and seventeen days—or don't you listen? I was here at the beginning with Frederix. The others went on to better things or were replaced over the last few semesters."

"Frederix?"

"A prestigious role for him."

"That was over five years ago… he's the only one who's not moved on?"

"I think the Company doesn't like him either."

"I've heard a few things about Frederix. Anything you want to add?"

Elbaz smiled, his bloodless lips revealing nicotine stained teeth. "You were way off the mark accusing Trinny. We are all mega-brains, but Lunn's is off the scale. And more than that, she's canny. She saw through Frederix straightaway. Offia is too practical, too streetwise to get involved with that idiot. I've observed Anton over time. He plays the relaxed, social chameleon, hiding behind his role of Director. Occasionally the mask slips."

"So where do you think the underwear came from?"

"I wouldn't put it past the Director to dress up once in a while. He's the repressed type. He probably gets off on it." He lets out another dark laugh. "Now, are you done?"

"You say Chen spent a lot of time in your desert dome?"

"You want to go see?"

The thought of that open space is a little worrying, but I'm here on an investigation. "There might be something of use. A clue perhaps."

Elbaz smiles for the first time since I've met him. Gone is the tense loner, in his place is someone more secure. "Sure. To be honest, it feels good to get some of that off my chest."

"A death sentence is difficult to live with."

"A death sentence would be easier." He laughs—a grim sound that comes from the back of his throat. "You should take the tour while you're here."

"I don't have the time. And besides, this place is not for me. It's too… too alien. That forest I came through—all those trees and insects gave me the heebie-jeebies."

Hassan's snake-like eyes peer at me as if I'm the alien. "You want to see insects, then I suggest you take a visit to my rainforest. It's my crowning glory… or it was."

"No thanks."

"You're not even tempted?"

"It's not my thing. And didn't you hear me? I don't have the time."

If Elbaz is disappointed, he doesn't show it. "Come on then."

We stand and walk down a wide roadway, entering an arch of golden and yellow-leafed oaks. Elbaz drones on about these massive outlandish growths and also about spruce, alders, birch, chestnuts and elms. They mean a lot to the guy, but to me? They are just nonsensical words. I couldn't care less—trees, one and all, are ugly and monstrous. I can't find it in myself to appreciate them. They may be 'natural'—whatever that means any more—but they are not natural to me. I prefer them as digivids.

The desert dome is directly opposite where I came in. We enter the now familiar plastic curtains, walk down another short tunnel and emerge into the dry heat of Elbaz's desert area. The temperature is intoxicating, surrounding me in a searing blanket of hot, thick air. The light is brighter—harsher and full of contrasting tones. Unlike the other domes I've seen, the hemisphere walls are clearly visible. As are two further exits. No attempt made to hide the grey, featureless curve. Somehow, that relaxes me.

Finely etched sand dunes cross the dome at an angle as if created by a desert breeze. An oasis—an explosion of green—sits in the centre.

Elbaz slides forward, controlled and even more snakelike, and I follow him. Not to the oasis, which I now see surrounds a pool of deepest azure, but towards a high dune.

"His spot is over the other side."

Ten minutes later, we reach the top of the dune and finally, I feel some of the chill leave my bones. The exertion is tiring, though rewarding. The area below sits in a depression. Standing there, like a peculiarly shaped marching band, are rows and rows of man-sized cactus plants splendid in their symmetry. Some are in bloom—blue and pink with many canopy-like flowers, others seemingly covered in fluff-like hair.

"I designed the cacti," Elbaz says dispassionately. "Engineered to act as water and air reservoirs in environmental extremes. They can survive the worst of heat and cold. They'd even last outside in space—for a while. The flowers are an affectation. They reproduce asexually. But blossoms are my calling card."

A thought occurs to me. "About your flowers—just what are those black blooms I saw back in the evergreen dome… in the forest clearing?"

Elbaz stops, seemingly taken aback by my question, his eyes narrowing again until all I can see of them is the glittering reflection of the dome's harsh UV light. "You noticed them, huh?" he says, wiping the sheen of sweat from his forehead and straightening his hair band.

"Mainly their smell," I reply with a covering half-laugh. I appear to have hit another nerve.

"Like I said, flowers are my thing—one of my many experiments."

The hydroponics expert has a secret. If my Skilled senses are telling me anything, it's that. Part of me is expecting to glimpse something more in the man. His intention. A poker player's tell, though again I get nothing. I'm frustrated and a little annoyed. It's as if I'm operating on half power.

We walk down the steep slope, disturbing sand that cascades around our feet in flurries and I soon realise these cacti are enormous in size. Twice my height and many times my width. I shy away from them.

"They can't hurt you," Elbaz says. "Not unless you prick yourself." He stops at a boulder. "Chen used to sit here for hours on end."

I do a search of the area while Elbaz stares on. Not that I know what I'm looking for. A clue perhaps?

Anything to get this investigation started. Some indication that this is more than a dumb suicide. I find only sand. "I'm done here," I say finally, turning to go.

Elbaz puts out a restraining hand on my shoulder and spins me around. His eyes stare into mine. "Don't tell anyone about me, okay?"

"About you being a dead man walking?"

He nods.

"I can't promise that," I say, thinking 'you and me both'.

He lets me go, his hand balling into a fist, although the cold anger leaves his eyes. "Just don't."

"Like I said, I can't promise anything. But, if it helps, I'm no blabbermouth. Okay?"

"Yeah, I suppose so."

"Good, now I need to get out of here."

jelinek

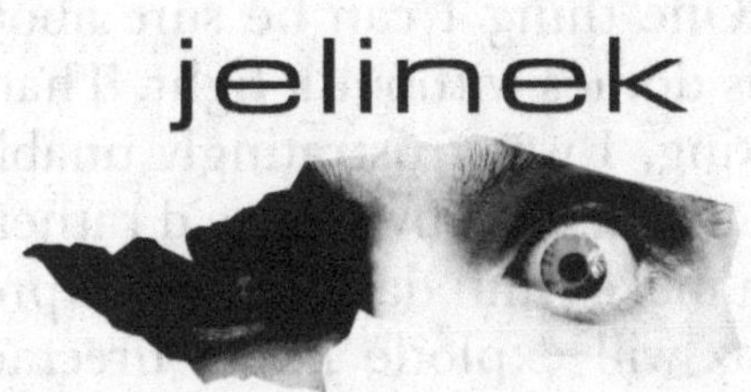

AFTER THE repeated cold of Elbaz's evergreen conifer dome, I'm chilled to the bone once again. Offia said this constant feeling of cold might last for up to six months. At the moment, I don't even have six hours. Precious minutes have slipped away while I've been chatting to the tree-hugger and I'm no closer to solving this puzzle. Yet I can't rush. I have to take things one step at a time.

What do I know? Not much, other than Offia is a certified flirt and, if I am to believe him, Elbaz's fantastic domes are soon to be closed down. I think back to the hydroponics expert. It's said that condemned men experience a clarity of vision and purpose. That they have the ability to push aside what the rest of us find important. To rise above the mundane concepts of retribution and small-mindedness. That they have moments of revelation denied to those living their lives from day to day. Not so Elbaz. In him, I sense a base desire to settle old scores. He's dangerous, yet the only thing he seemed to hate was the Company—a faceless entity. It may be argued that I presently represent the Company, but again, I didn't sense any personal loathing from him, although I could tell he was waiting to see what I had to say. One thing I can be sure about—Elbaz won't leave his domes without a fight. That's not my abilities speaking, I was frustratingly unable to look inside the man. Still, it's obvious he'd rather die than do that, which makes him dangerous but predictable. One day Elbaz will explode like a firecracker. The upshot? Faking a suicide just isn't his style.

There's also no news from Offia regarding those blood tests. I hope she is taking this seriously.

I make my way back to Habitation and nod to Bill who is still doing chores in the canteen.

"How goes the investigation?" he asks with a playful rise of his eyebrows.

"I found a couple of smokes."

"You did? Cool."

I locate the hatchway to Chen Jelinek's quarters, his rooms are sealed as Frederix told me. I use the eye-scanner and the door opens.

Darkness.

The lights are automatic and should come on as soon as anyone enters. The same sensors switching them off if they detect no human presence. The base is not power-starved, but this is protocol for all Company areas, which makes sense when energy is at a premium—like on a ship or a space station.

I wave my arms a few times to no effect before giving up and going back to the canteen where I get a smiling Bill to fetch me a torch. Minutes later, we both enter Chen's rooms. I weighed up whether or not to include the kid in my search and decided it would work in my favour. He's useful in a practical way. And besides, I like him.

"Have you been in here before?" I ask Bill, shining the torch into his face like an interrogation.

"Nope. Never set a foot in anyone's quarters on Karst base. Everyone is too paranoid—I'm sure you must've noticed that already. This kinda feels like trespassing, don't you think?"

"Trespassing is pretty much my job description. You ever let anyone in your quarters?"

The question seems to throw him. "No," he says rather too quickly, his brown eyes flashing while his head twitches to the left and right. He's lying. I can read him easily. If the gossip was true concerning him and Trinny, it's likely she'd sworn him to silence. I decide not to push the point. This investigation isn't about what Bill does in his spare time. At least, I don't think it is.

We both flick our torches around and reveal an identical room to that of the Director. A manufactured living-module printed from the asteroid's raw material and glued into place. The Company is not unimaginative, just efficient. Then again, this is the Zetas-Karst Laboratories. From what I can glimpse of them, the fitments are top-notch. The only thing similar to Frederix's quarters is the shape.

The place is a mess and smells bad. Half-full cups of coffee, green with mould, and plates of unfinished food litter the floor. Discarded clothes lie here and there. The rooms of a teenager, not a respected forty-something scientist.

On top of all the mess are hundreds of paper sheets—the floors and walls are covered in them. And when I say 'hundreds' I mean just that.

"What the hell?" says Bill, kicking his way through the accumulated detritus.

I grasp one of the sheets of paper. Four words are printed repeatedly: 'I am Chen Jelinek'. The last thing Chen said to Elbaz, the words the hydroponic expert tried to hide from the others. I pick up another sheet. The same. Every page covered with this curious statement. Most are computer printouts, others written in a shaky hand.

I am Chen Jelinek. I am Chen Jelinek. I am Chen Jelinek. I am Chen Jelinek. I am Chen Jelinek. I am Chen Jelinek. I am Chen Jelinek. I am Chen Jelinek. I am Chen Jelinek. I am Chen Jelinek. I am Chen Jelinek. I am Chen Jelinek. I am Chen Jelinek. I am Chen...

"Any idea what the hell this is about?" Bill asks, his voice tight and a little reedy.

"You okay?"

"Sure. I just didn't realise Chen was so far gone." He points the torch under his chin, throwing dark shadows over his smooth, rounded face. "I knew the man had issues—we all did—but nothing like this. The poor guy must've been really suffering."

"He sure was."

Bill plays the beam around Chen's room again. "So why are we here? You after anything in particular?"

"I'm looking for a note, something that might help explain Chen's death. Or a clue or three. This makes no sense."

I grab at more sheets. They are the same. I wonder if this is a distraction placed here by a possible murderer, to try and knock me off the scent. If that's the case, it's a pretty damn impressive diversion filling out all these sheets of paper. I shake my head in the dark. No matter what I might think, I can't ignore what's in front of me. I have to admit that there's a very strong possibility Chen was off his rocker. The kind of behaviour of someone seriously ill—the kind of behaviour that may indicate his death was indeed suicide.

I pat Bill on the shoulder and go over to Chen's desk. "Do you know your way around a data-centre?"

"Sure, my… um… area of expertise. Processors and that stuff. But there's no access without Chen's physical presence. These things are bio-locked, with many other more complex ways of—"

The data-centre flickers into life. Chen's home screen displayed.

"Oh," says Bill. "That's unexpected."

"We're in?"

"Looks like it. He must have removed the security protocols… I've never heard of such a thing."

"I'm after a note. Anything that might explain this as a suicide—see what you can find."

"You don't still think he was murdered?"

"What I think doesn't matter a jot. I'm after evidence. And suicide notes are not always genuine."

Reading another's data-centre without permission is not only a terrible betrayal of trust, it's also illegal. Akin to breaking and entering. If Bill is feeling ill-at-ease as he slides into the chair, I don't sense it. As for me? I'm used to this kind of larceny.

Was I really in hibernation on a colonial ship, shipped off to go play farmer at the farthest reaches of the galaxy? I can't remember anything about that. About the reasons why I chose such a path. Solitude would certainly suit me, but a farming life? No. This is where I'm truly alive. Investigating.

Bill's eyes widen. "Christ!"

I am Chen Jelinek. I am Chen…

The same four words suddenly cover the screen. Bill pulls up file after file. All identical.

"Has he been hacked?" I ask. "Could that be it?"

Bill's answer is to pull up a directory. "You see these personal idents? They're biometric and impossible to compromise. He did this by himself."

"There's kilo-quads of data. Must've taken him months. Is this what he was doing instead of his gravity experiments?"

Bill let's out a long sigh. "Sure looks that way."

A full search of the rest of the cluttered quarters reveals nothing other than more mess—the man was living like an animal. We both leave Chen's rooms perplexed. I close and lock the door behind me.

"Do you want a coffee?" Bill asks, subdued.

I check my wafer:

2 hours, 43 minutes remaining.

I'm rapidly running out of time. Sod it! My organs might be about to expire, but a cup of char is just what I need, particularly after the whisky I've consumed. I nod and we both go over to the canteen.

A jug on a hot plate throws out delicious aromas and soon, he's pouring me a cupful. He sits down next to me, his smooth brown hands cradling a personalised mug with the words 'WORLD'S WORST BOSS' spelled out in large capital letters. The irony isn't wasted upon me.

I break the silence. "Did Chen show any sign of mental illness?"

"He killed himself... I'd say that was a big indicator."

"Other than his... supposed suicide?"

Bill sips from his mug. "Like everyone said. He was a bit of a jerk. He'd argue over petty stuff."

"Give me an example."

The kid shrugs. "Nothing specific. Just people crap."

"Did anyone go out of their way to wind him up?"

"Maybe Ackermann."

I think back to the large, angry robotician and smile at the memory of stabbing him in the hand. I enjoyed bringing him down a peg or two.

"After the first power-outage, Ackermann became particularly annoyed," says Bill carefully, as if afraid of being overheard. "There were a few slanging matches. Nothing serious. But everyone agreed with him. Those power cuts were a real problem."

"I don't get it," I say, slurping a mouthful of delicious coffee, part of me still hankering after the addition of a drop of whisky. "The Company brought me out of hypersleep to come and investigate this thing. Which raises two questions. Firstly, what was so important about Chen Jelinek to warrant an investigation? Especially after the Company sacked him only hours before. And secondly, why put one of the Skilled, an adept investigator, on the case? I'm still a little bit groggy, but from what I remember, and from what you've told me, the Skilled are a kind of elite."

Bills eyebrows furrow above his mug. "That's true," he says, putting the heavy cup back on the table.

"Regardless whether Chen Jelinek killed himself or not, there's a deeper mystery on this base. Has to be. Why else would the Company send me here?" I said pretty much the same thing to Offia. This time, the words sound hollow, as if I'm trying to fool myself. I can't be wrong on this. I just can't. "My investigation isn't about Chen. It never was."

"If your theory is correct," says Bill, picking up his mug again and taking a thoughtful sip, "what's this enquiry really about?"

It's my turn to furrow my eyebrows. "Well, my coffee-making friend, there is only one way to find out." I take a final chug of the bitter, but refreshing liquid and stand up. "Time to go screw with Ackermann."

"Good luck!"

bluster

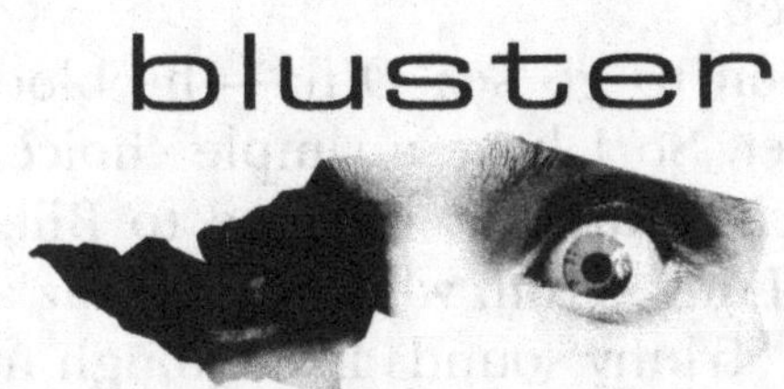

I ENTER the cramped Karst Base corridors again and think about what I know already. Chen was not of sound mind when he died. His papers and files written with those four words was proof of that. And if Elbaz wasn't lying, Chen's last words could've only been a manic request for help. I've no idea what Offia is going to tell me after she's analysed Chen's blood, but my gut says she'll find nothing. Which means I'm back to square one. This investigation is turning into one big dead end.

I feel the wafer nestled next to my skin inside my tightfitting spacesuit. I don't take out the handheld. I don't need to. Time is slipping by—I can sense the change in my body, my cells swirling within a sea of toxins, drowning one-by-one. My organs starting to struggle against this rising tide.

"There's more to this!" I gasp in frustration. There has to be. Why else send me here? But—

I live for truth.

The phrase shines brightly in my consciousness like the bright comet I glimpsed in the cold harshness of space. A beacon of light where all was dark. And like a mantra, I repeat that expression in my mind. It gives a sense of peace and allows me to concentrate on my next step.

It's too soon to go see Offia—the blood results won't be in yet. So I have a simple choice. I either visit Frank Ackermann, as I voiced to Bill, or drop in on Trinny Lunn. From what both Elbaz and Offia have told me, Trinny sounds like a tough nut. A nut I'm not quite ready to crack. Ackermann is a nothing more than a bag of hot air. I decide to go and call on him first and put some additional wind up him.

The corridors are quiet and suffocating. Part of me hankers for escape. Maybe that's why I was on my way to one of those colony planets. I'm no farmer, far from it—my experience inside Elbaz's domes has taught me that if nothing else, but I can see the attraction of such a life. No humans for miles. Just my land and me. Other people are messy. Annoying. Too difficult to live with. Running my own farm sounds idyllic—but I know myself. It wouldn't be enough. And would I ever be free of the Company? I doubt it.

Before I realise, I'm standing outside Frank Ackermann's lab. His name blinks erratically on the display, fizzing on and off. I press the chime. No reply. I try again. Nothing.

I put my eye to the scanner. The hatchway opens with a hiss and a few clacks and clunks and I walk inside. A short stub of a corridor leads to another dome. Silent. Half the size of Chen's, yet still large.

To be honest, I'm surprised. I was expecting the hum of machinery, the snap and hum of robotics,

Ackermann in the middle of some vital work—the white-hot heat of top-end Company research. Instead, the dome is quiet.

"Ackermann!"

Enormous lifting rigs rear above me—like the long dead bones of metal beasts. Other machines seem abandoned and untended—half-completed sculptures of steel and carbon, their innards spilling out as coils of wire and broken data-wafers. A robotic graveyard rather than a birthplace.

"Ackermann!"

I saunter towards the centre of his laboratory, passing more disassembled machines. The whole place appears to be a shrine to the unfinished and the undone. What in space is going on here?

I spot a pair of legs sticking out from under a metal canopy. I rush over, fearing the worst. I find Frank Ackermann lying on a makeshift bed, asleep and snoring quietly.

Next to him is half a pint of vodka. I pick up the bottle and swig down a couple of mouthfuls. Cheap. Bitter with no depth. I take one more chug of the harsh liquor and pour the rest over Ackerman's face. His gargantuan head twitches but he remains unconscious. There's nothing for it, I kick him hard and he coughs and splutters into life.

"Wakey, wakey!" I say with a smile upon my lips. This is going to be fun.

Pig-like eyes, free from his glasses, stare up at me. I notice a tremor in them. Nystagmus—*dancing eyes*. The effect makes him appear shifty and underhand. "What the hell?"

"We need to talk, you fat drunken pig."

"Get out of here!" His reedy voice is almost a squeak. He rolls over on to his mammoth belly and pushes himself up onto stubby arms.

"I'm afraid that isn't going to happen," I say, kicking him again. Nothing nasty, just a playful tap on his immense butt. He crumples onto his mattress, the air escaping from his lungs in a loud gasp.

"You bastard!" he manages to croak.

Ackermann struggles back up and I allow him to raise his vast bulk onto his long, yet sturdy legs. He towers over me, his fat face purple with rage. He wants to hit me—I see the anger in his twitching grey eyes and the tremble of his quivering flesh. I almost want him to lose his cool. I'd love a reason to kick his arrogant ass around his excuse for a lab, but he controls himself.

"That was the last of my vodka you fool!" he shouts, glaring at the empty bottle.

"Yeah, a real shame to waste such top booze."

He strides over to his desk, pulling at his lab coat and wiping the vodka from his face. He flicks his data-centre into life with an angry wave of one of his immense hands. "Director!" he barks.

No answer.

"Director! This is Ackermann! Director!"

"How about you stop this ridiculous performance and talk to me."

Ackermann acts as if I'm not there. "Director!" He spins around and heads for the door. Unable to help myself, I trip him up. He falls heavily, knocking into a chair with a loud clatter. I roll him over and sit on his chest. "Are you going to talk to me, or do I have to beat up on you? Your choice."

I'm half his size and in my present condition, only a third of his weight, though I can hold him down easily. He can't lift the combined poundage of us both.

"Get off me!"

I shake my head.

"I'm warning you, Vatic!"

"I'm going nowhere until you calm down."

I let Ackermann struggle until he tires himself out. Like breaking an angry colt. Or, more accurately, an overweight, annoyed charger well past its prime. Finally, his struggles cease and he lies back puffing, out of breath, his face clammy with sweat.

"You ready to talk yet?"

The big man says nothing.

"I'm gonna keep sitting here all day until you get some sense in that humongous head of yours."

"Yes, yes! All right! Now remove yourself!"

"I will, if you'll calm down and talk to me."

"You have my word!" he blurts, shouting. He's defeated and knows it.

I clamber off his belly and offer him a hand. He takes it in an enormous spatula that dwarfs my own. I wonder if he's going to pull me over, but the fight has gone out of him. I drag him to wobbly feet and he stumbles back to his desk to sit heavily in a chair that's seen better days.

"I suppose that idiot Frederix gave you permission to enter my lab, huh?"

"I work for the Company. Frederix has no authority over me or what I choose to do. But you already know that."

Ackermann digests the information for a few seconds, although it's clear I've finally impressed him. "What do you want?" he says, rubbing at his injured hand.

"Chen died, or don't you remember."

"And good riddance to the little shit."

"Before we get to him, you can tell me what you're doing in this lab… or more to the point. What you've not been doing. Back in the canteen, you gave every impression you were a busy man."

Ackermann's shoulders jerk forward in a thick, fleshy shrug. "That's my business. It has no bearing on why that idiot, Chen, offed himself."

"I beg to differ. So I'll ask you again… what's going on here?"

The big man's chin drops to his chest, squashing out his immense neck. One hand grabs his glasses from the desk and jams them onto his face. "I just don't see why—"

"Tell me!"

"I've not worked since I got here. Call it early retirement."

"The Company wouldn't pay for all of this without results."

A scowl crosses Ackermann's features. "Do you think me stupid?"

I say nothing, deciding to let the big man speak.

"I am producing work. Great work. It's just that my research is being done… *by someone else.*"

"Explain?"

"If you knew anything about robotics, you'd know

I'm the bees-knees. The head-honcho. The top dog. I personally revolutionised the field. That's not conceit—I have the awards to prove it. And there are plenty of young scientists out there vying with one another to be my legitimate successor. So why shouldn't I use them."

"You're a fake?"

"They do the leg-work and I receive the credit. In return, they benefit from my advice and more importantly, my recommendation. I'm the real deal. You don't get to where I am without bloody hard work. I've earned this."

"And the Company doesn't know about this little arrangement?"

Ackermann lifts his head, a smile parting his face. "Of course not. And that's the way it's going to stay."

"So all your bluster is for show only?"

"Not for show, they expect it."

"Doesn't a man like you become bored?"

"I tinker," he says, glancing over to the half-finished projects and machines. "I'll retire in a few years. This is a sort of practice run."

"And the vodka?"

"So what if I drink? That's nobody's business but my own."

"That wasn't your last half-pint, was it?"

"What are you getting at?"

"If I get Offia to analyse your blood, it'd be forty percent proof. You're a boozer. Probably borderline alcoholic. That's the real reason why other people are working for you, isn't it? You're washed up. Finished."

"I drink as much as I want, when I want. I've

earned it and others are more than willing to do the leg-work for me. So why not?"

"If that's the case, Chen's work didn't affect your experiments. You were lying back in the canteen."

A nod of his mammoth head. "Just bullshit," he squeaks. "What I'm good at."

I take in the information, the beginning of a smile playing upon my lips. A pattern is emerging. Elbaz waiting for the axe, his work side-lined, Chen unable to deliver on his promises and now Ackermann revealed as a drunken faker. "Did you have anything at all to do with Chen? Did you ever speak?"

"Chen turned up under a cloud. Gossip said he was ruined. That he'd become a fantasist. He'd promised too much and couldn't deliver."

"You say that was before he arrived here?"

"Yeah. That was odd. The Company are not known for giving second chances."

"You think that's what it was? A second chance?"

"Maybe. Force field manipulation is one of the Company's Holy Grails. They've been after it for decades."

"You know about his research? I thought everyone's work was secret."

"Not the ins-and-outs, although we all have an inkling what the others are up to. Apart from Elbaz and those damn domes of his. He says anyone can get access, though that's not true. He's never let me anywhere near them."

"What do you know of their work?" I ask, not letting him distract me.

Ackermann's wet lips purse for a second. "Nothing

really. I'd go see Frederix, he's always hinting about this and that. Fishing for information. He likes to play the puppet-master."

"That's what everyone seems to be telling me."

"He won't take kindly to you stealing his thunder."

"He doesn't have a choice. Now… is there anything else you want to tell me about Chen? About his death? Or about this base and the people here?"

"Only that he must've killed himself."

"You're that sure?"

The man sits back in his chair, the thin metal creaking under the added pressure. "I suppose it's possible someone got to him," he says like the thought had never previously crossed his mind.

I'm intrigued. "What do you mean *someone got to him?*"

Ackermann pushes himself to shaky feet and ambles over to a large cabinet. He opens the door revealing more bottles of Vodka. He self-consciously grabs a half pint, fills a glass and takes a thoughtful swig. "The Company and its major players are shrewd," he says, with all trace of his earlier bluster now gone, "conniving and pretty much without conscience. Who knows how someone could have made him do it. A promise of money to a loved one, perhaps. Although the man was unlovable. But that's clutching at straws—Chen had nothing to offer. No collateral. Logic says he must've have killed himself. And besides, what possible motive could there be to bump off the little idiot?"

It's not the answer I'm after, although so far, I've come up with no other explanation. "Anything else?"

A slow shake of his head. "I've told you everything I know."

I'm annoyed. This is not what I was expecting. Other than the realisation that Elbaz, Chen and now Ackermann were redundant as scientists, this conversation has gotten me nowhere. "Okay," I say.

"So you're done?"

I nod.

Ackermann slams his glass down with a bang. "Good. Now piss off!"

We stare at each other, eye to eye for a few moments. "I may want to speak to you again. Please don't make it as difficult, understand?"

Ackermann rears up in front of me. "I said piss off."

war

THE CRAMPED corridors feel even more suffocating as I make my way to Lunn's lab. I depress the chime and, almost immediately, the door opens with a hiss and a click. I walk inside a room the colour of cerulean. Blue and silver hues dominate walls that are straight and beautiful—crackling with the sparkle of electricity and life. This is unlike any other lab or any other part of this base I've visited today. No prefabricated dome. Instead, her lab is elongated and airy.

The hatch closes behind me automatically. A delicate breeze blows around an array of linked data-stacks, standing like tall, black beehives. I walk through them, shivering, until I reach the far end and a collection of glass-walled, roofless chambers and rooms. In one of them, I spy the diminutive form of Trinny Lunn.

Back in the harsh illumination of the canteen, her face was cast with shadows and hollows. Here, under the somewhat flattering light of her lab, she is revealed as a high cheek-boned beauty. It's rare to see someone so white, the colour fell out of favour over two centuries ago. Trinny's skin has the tone and quality of alabaster. She stands stiff and straight—petite, centred, busy—a tight-fitting lab coat doing nothing to hide her delicate curves. She's in here on her own, yet dresses to please.

Is she expecting me, or does she always dress so agreeably?

Her bright green, crystal eyes sparkle with intent—framed by thick, shoulder length, flaxen hair. Trinny's features complement each other. The result of a lot of work and Company dollars or she's naturally endowed—either way she must be using anti-aging drugs. Despite her fascinating looks, she cannot hide her age. It pokes through in the delicate lines around her eyes and mouth, in the slight hollowness of her cheeks and eye-sockets. The woman is seventy-three, yet she passes as someone in her mid to late forties. I'm impressed on a number of levels.

She is chatting into a data-centre suspended from the ceiling. A closer inspection reveals the machine is connected to a wafer-stack covering the entire roof area and can reposition itself anywhere in the lab. A vast piece of computing power. Trinny Lunn beckons me with a delicate white-hand.

I open the glass door to her cubicle and enter. "I've come to—"

She raises her hand again and whispers into her data-centre. I hear another voice replying—computerised, warm and full of bouncing tones, but I cannot make out any of the words, although I'm sure my name was mentioned.

I examine Lunn for a second time. Her lower legs

are uncovered except for short white socks and high-heeled, ankle-boots. Her calves are small and well-proportioned, the skin unblemished. I'm pleased to note she is just under my height. It feels good to be taller than a woman. A primeval thing maybe? I can change my stature if needed, like most things to do with appearance. I'm happy in my skin although, sadly, that's all I am at the moment. That and a little bone. My eyes linger longer than they should.

Trinny flicks a disapproving look in my direction. "I'm wearing underwear, if that's what you're looking for," she says with a gentle snort. "Hello Vatic," she adds, offering me a slender hand.

I take her fingers in mine without thinking.

"I've been expecting you," she says, letting go almost immediately.

"I guess the undergarment I found was not yours, huh?"

A quick shake of her head. "You were making a power play back in the canteen—seeing who reacted, who didn't. I understand that. I can't say I was pleased with your accusation, though watching the Director squirm put a smile on my face." Her voice is quiet yet powerful, containing an attractive rasp.

"So I'm forgiven?"

Trinny's wide upturned lips lift to reveal an array of perfect, whitened teeth. "You are only doing your job, which I respect. If more people did their jobs properly, the Company would be twice as efficient." She tilts her head to one side and looks at me, reminding me of a curious bird. "You like your profession, don't you?"

"I'm in the odd position of not actually knowing

if I do or not," I answer, wondering why I'm suddenly being amenable. "I was woken out of hypersleep to come here. Most of my memory has gone. So far, I'm working on autopilot."

"Is that why you look like you do?" Trinny indicates my emaciated frame with a flick of her fingers. "Why on Earth were you in hypersleep?"

"I dunno. My best guess is that I was running away. From what? I'm not quite sure."

"I have to say I'm less than awestruck coming face-to face with a Skilled. I expected… well… something more."

I'm again aware of my emaciated appearance. I'm not at my best—far from it. Trinny has insight, she somehow guessed that narcissism is my weak spot. A way to get at me. I'm vain, that much is for sure. And I've a thing for sexy, intelligent women—which can't be good—any which way I look at it. "Tell me, do you think Chen committed suicide?"

Trinny pauses for a long time. "That's for you to work out isn't it?"

"I suppose it is. But indulge me. What does your gut say?"

Trinny takes a step back, placing a single, thin hand on the curve of her slender hip. "Tell me everything you know about Nanobiology."

I shrug. "Only that the technology was supposed to be the big thing, until people started dying. A fringe science, championed over two-hundred years ago, as some sort of universal cure-all. The reality was entirely different. Human physiology differed significantly from one person to the other, so much so that the side effects were too random and dangerous. Treatments and procedures still endure today in a minimal form—although there's a stigma attached to them. Quite frankly, people don't like or want little robots creating havoc within their systems."

I'm impressed with myself. I can't seem to remember the many details of my own life, yet the potted history of nano-technology isn't a problem for me. If my little lecture upsets her, Trinny doesn't show it.

"But what do you know about micro-biomechanical theory? About molecular design and bio-array implementation? About quantum surgery?"

"Nothing. I'm no expert. That's your job."

"Exactly. So why do you think I'll know anything about your area of expertise? What my gut may or may not feel regarding Chen Jelinek means—if you will excuse the phrase—*Jack shit*. You can't do my job and I certainly can't and don't want to do yours.

Even from these first few exchanges, I can see Trinny Lunn is a force to be reckoned with. I'm determined to not let her intimidate me. I'm in charge here. "My job is pretty straightforward. I ask questions and you answer. If you don't answer me? Well—you're intelligent enough to work out the consequences."

"That assumes I have pertinent replies. Any speculation on my part is just that—speculation. I can't see how my conjecture can possibly be useful to this investigation. I honestly believe your time will be better spent interrogating the others."

"You're saying you don't have an opinion either way?"

"I'm saying that what I think hardly matters."

"That's not an answer."

"It's the best you'll get out of me. Your job is to make deductions, to use your inbuilt empathy. Despite appearances, you are one of the Skilled. So go away and... *be skilled.*"

She's centred, in control. Threatening Trinny with the Company, with shutting down her labs won't work. She requires an entirely different approach. I lean forward and kiss her on the lips. Again, I do this from instinct—she wanted empathy, so I give it to her.

Our tongues meet and we share a perfunctory, if not intimate moment, after which, we part.

Trinny tries to appear unfazed, yet I can see I've broken through her hard exterior. A faint blush of red flushes her high cheekbones and her green eyes sparkle with anger. She was not expecting this from me.

"Am I now supposed to swoon and act like putty in your fingers?" she says too quickly. "Because that won't work. Not with Trinny Lunn."

I decide to drive my advantage. "I didn't notice you pull away."

Trinny searches my face for a few seconds, her eyes coming to rest on my own. She seems impatient. "I understand the technique—it's very simple to say the least—you're trying to distract me. As I've said, I know nothing pertinent to the investigation. Your time is best spent elsewhere. Now if you will indulge me I've prepared you a little—"

"I decide how this investigation is run. Not you. I'm here on direct Company orders. Some might argue that now, on this base… I am the Company."

She shakes her head vehemently. "Don't get above yourself, Vatic. You're nothing more than their bloodhound."

"Maybe. But the Company gave me carte blanche to do what is needed to find the underlying cause of Chen Jelinek's suicide. And believe me—I will fuck with you and everyone who gets in my way. Do you understand?"

Crystal green eyes stare into my own again, as if Trinny is trying to divine what's inside of me, although she is no empath.

"Answer me!"

Trinny's eyes linger for a moment longer. I can't read her properly. I don't need to. It's obvious she's neither impressed nor intimidated by me.

"Okay, Vatic. You win. Let's finish this quickly. What do you want to know?"

I admit it, I didn't expect her to fold so easily. I'm thrown for a second.

"Cat got your tongue?"

"Did you like Chen?" I ask finally.

"Did I like Chen?" She repeats the words like it's the dumbest question she's ever heard. Her eyes narrow to a glitter of green, her head tilting to one side again in an attitude of mock contemplation. "Mmm. That's a tricky one."

"Just answer me."

"I have no feelings either way."

I say nothing, waiting for her to continue.

"Chen made some kind of breakthrough in his field early in his career—or he stole someone's work—and was living off that success ever since. As to anything else he was mixed up with? I've no idea. Nor do I care."

"What if his situation was desperate?" I ask. "Would he take his own life?"

Trinny takes a while to answer. "That's for you to divine. But desperate measures are often taken by those besieged by desperation, if that was indeed the case."

"Did you notice anything odd about him?"

A short laugh escapes from the back of her throat. "I talked to him maybe once or twice. Got the measure of him. After that, it was almost as if he didn't exist. Apart from the power problems."

"They affected your work?"

"Not really, everything in my lab is backed up, with multiple inbuilt redundant systems. I even have my own energy supply."

I'm not surprised—her research area is a significant cut above anything I've seen today. "Back in the canteen you seemed as annoyed as the rest?"

"I don't want anyone to know I've got fringe benefits. That'd piss off those other egos."

So far, out of everyone I've talked to, Chen's power outages only affected Offia. As a motive for homicide, it was tentative at best. And now, after talking to the remaining three scientists, murder seemed even less likely. "What do you do here?" I ask. "With your nanites?"

"Brilliant stuff, mostly."

"Just give me the highlights."

"As I said, I work in nanobiology. I believe we

abandoned the technology before the field was truly understood. All we need is a breakthrough, a way to make this tek available to everyone, without those unfortunate side-effects you mentioned. We can cure millions."

"And have you made that advance?"

Trinny goes silent for a moment. "My research here is nearly finished."

After chatting to Elbaz and Ackermann, I'm wondering if her work is just as redundant. She's hiding something. There's nothing wrong in that, nothing intrinsically suspicious—people hide things all the time. If we didn't, we'd end up killing each other. She's been trying to get rid of me since I arrived in her lab. "Why aren't you telling me everything?"

"And why do you believe that's what I'm doing?"

"Instinct."

Trinny runs a slender hand over her neck and again fixes me with her green eyes. "Let me be absolutely clear. I do not want to hinder this investigation in any way. Sure, there's hidden stuff I know about—you probably sense that. But, and this is as sincere as I can make it, you're wasting your time with me. I can't help you."

A beep from my wafer. I step back to examine the screen. A message from Offia: *Results are in. Come to my lab.*

I wonder why she doesn't simply tell me over the com. I should go over there now, yet Trinny intrigues me. I feel there's more to come from her. "What were you doing when I came in?"

For the first time since this conversation started,

Trinny appears impressed. "Actually, I was chatting to Christopher—about you. I set him a chore after Bill told me you were having a few memory problems. A little surprise to help you along the way."

"Christopher?"

"My data-centre."

I flick my eyes up at the ceiling taken over by her 'Christopher' and whistle. "That's quite some computing power you have at your disposal."

"Size isn't everything."

I'm expecting a flirty glance or at least a cheeky raise of her lips. Nothing. There's obviously more to what she's saying than simple human repartee. "You say, you've chatted to Bill?"

"Why yes, is there a problem?"

"Are you close to him?"

Her eyebrows raise. "You can probably sense that me and Bill are more than friends," she says carefully, looking away from me. "You Skilled have an aptitude in those areas."

I nod, deciding not to tell her I've sensed nothing of the sort—that it was Offia who guessed her and Bill's secret. "I'm not sure who's the lucky one, you or Bill."

Trinny gives me a confused look before activating her data-centre. "Christopher?"

The background hum of electronics increases for a second and a voice, full of bass tones—both soothing and commanding—fills the room. "Yes, Ma'am?"

"Christopher is not connected to my work directly, although he's a valuable assistant," Trinny says to me, like a proud mother introducing her child. "My helper so to speak. Christopher… say hello to Vatic."

"Good afternoon, Mister Vatic."

"It's Vatic," I spit, unable to hide my distaste, "just Vatic."

Trinny seems surprised. "You don't like computers?"

I shake my head. "They cause more problems than they solve."

"You can't really believe that… *can you?*"

"Remember back in the early days? When true artificial sentience was the goal. Another Holy Grail?"

"I may be older than I look, but not that old."

"But you know your history. The many philosophical arguments about slavery and sentient rights and if, one day, machines would own themselves."

"What are you getting at?"

"They were premature. True consciousness was as elusive as it was sought after. As far as anyone can tell, it's impossible to make such a machine sentient… and there lies the problem. Modern machines, like your Christopher, may mimic human intelligence, may seem to respond intuitively, may engage and deduce, but he is not the real thing. Just one big dump of billions of off-and-on switches and nothing else—all at the control of the frail-minded stupid human at the other end."

If Trinny is insulted by my words, she doesn't show it. "All very much true, although I seem to be missing your point. Christopher can't actually think but he's a very useful research tool."

"I'm not denying such things are necessary. Super-brains run most of the Company's operations.

Artificial ganglion centres and mind-trusts control so many vital systems. Sure, they're needed. But why humanise them? Why make them into something they're not?"

"I should've realised you'd be like this."

"Like what?"

"You're an empath. You despise computers because you can't read them."

I shake my head. "Using a human interface makes it all the easier to commit any number of atrocities." I snap, aware of an irrational anger growing inside of me. I don't like computers, that much is for certain, although I'm unsure as to why.

"I can assure you I have no atrocities planned," Christopher says with a hint of humour, his booming, artificial voice filling the cubicle.

"I asked Christopher to do a little bit of background research," says Trinny with a small smile.

"About me?"

"Yes, Vatic," Christopher booms over the rich bass of the lab sound system. "But first let me say how honoured I am to meet such a distinguished war veteran."

"Wh—What?" I'm flummoxed, wrong-footed.

Trinny stands back, resting her weight on one, high-heeled boot. "So you were decorated in the Corporate Wars huh? I'm impressed. I thought at first the Company may have sent us a dud. Sounds like you are one of their top operatives."

My voice is a dull croak. "The war?"

"You don't remember?"

I shake my head.

"Christopher," Trinny orders. "Tell us more about Vatic's war record."

The booming voice continues. "Vatic. Born Twenty-Two Sixty-Two. At age nine, after the Decree of Genetic Manipulation, he was deemed an illegal entity and spent the next ten years in captivity, until the Decree was repealed. Vatic then entered Company employ, where he became a Skilled agent. At the outbreak of the Twenty-Two Ninety-Six Corporate Wars, he enlisted as a Special Operative. He is a holder of six medals of Collateral Warship, the Corporate Medal of Achievement and the Special Recognition Medal for services above and beyond the Company. Vatic holds the rank of Secondary Executive, and is responsible for three-million, four-hundred thousand and fifty-eight quantifiable kills. Was Tertiary Instigator at the Battle of Nairn and Primary Overseer in the Clean-Up Aftermath."

"Wow," Trinny says looking me up and down. "That's quite some record."

"Secondary Executive Vatic also played a vital part in the annexation of—"

"Shut it up!" I shout, as memories, hot like burning knives, stab into my mind.

"What?"

"I said shut the thing up!"

Trinny waves her hand and the disembodied voice stops. "You're a Goddamn hero."

Responsible for three-million, four-hundred thousand and fifty-eight quantifiable kills. Those words scythe into me.

Quantifiable kills.

I'm a murderer.

Three-million, four-hundred thousand and fifty-eight people. The numbers astound me. How could I possibly kill so many?

Another beep from the wafer. Offia again. "I'm going," I say to Trinny.

"You okay?"

I nod.

"Good. Now go do your job, soldier-boy!" Trinny shouts after me, making a salute.

shards

I LEAVE Trinny's lab feeling dizzy and disorientated. I finally collapse in a heap, my back to the cold corridor wall and close my eyes.

I'm no longer in the base, but standing on a building with a wide balcony. My viewpoint looks down into a yawning chasm full of churning machinery and belching gases, disappearing into the far distance. I recognize the monstrosity as a *Wormer*. A five-mile long cylinder of industrial, military processing hanging in space like an indolent whale. The concept is simple—add raw materials, asteroid debris and space junk at one end, and collect processed minerals and metals at the other. The thing was more complicated than that. And more often than not, used as simple biological waste disposal—if you know what I mean.

I take a deep breath of the heavy, ozone smelling air. The Wormer has its own atmosphere—a thin envelope allowing me to breathe and to observe an amazing starscape, although most of it is hidden by the cloud of dust these machines spew out—hanging in space like a polluted, stained comet.

The Milky Way, half-obscured, extends up and over my head, surrounded by a myriad of pinprick stars. Andromeda is beautiful set against such stark blackness. An astounding vista, but cold. I feel myself shivering.

I know I'm dreaming, that I'm still on Karst in the midst of an investigation with time running out, and yet my subconscious has brought me here. I've been in this place before. A room of nightmares. What happened here?

"Vatic?"

The voice is faraway, faint. A woman's voice. The timbre is familiar, painful. I can't answer, I mustn't answer.

"Vatic! Come inside. And close those damn doors, it's freezing."

I turn and stare back into what I recognise as a bedroom. I've seen this vista before, hundreds of times. A double bed sits against the far wall, a black satin over-sheet thrown onto the worn carpet, the bedclothes crumpled. I leave the balcony with its spectacular views, walk inside and close the doors, recognising fitments that seemed to have been seared into my brain: twin bedside lights each with an orange lampshade standing atop cupboards with chrome handles. A cabinet stacked with booze and littered with half-empty cocktail glasses. A large black and white print of a reclining woman smoking a stylised cigarette—her bright red lips the only colour. A crumpled blue dress lying on the floor next to an upturned, sling back shoe. A dressing table above which hangs a mirror with my reflection—not the pale excuse of a man I've grown to know over the past few hours—but an assured thirty-something. I'm wearing a black suit with an open-collared white shirt. Underneath, I glimpse the grey of a skinsuit. I'm muscular, taut—and dangerous. And those eyes… they sparkle and burn like twin, blue, angry suns. Bright and steely—manic with the fervour of truth and deserving retribution. I've seen this image of myself many times. It haunts me. I hate the man in the mirror. I hate who he is and what he's about to do.

"Vatic," the voice continues. "Fix me a drink while I'm getting ready."

I then notice the gun in my hand. Palm-coded, deadly.

"Vatic? Are you deaf?" A naked woman enters the room from the en-suite. Red hair flows from her head in a cascade of curls. Golden eyes stab out of her face. Eyes like my own. Haunted, wired, unnatural in colour. She's a Skilled. "What the hell is this?" she says calmly, her finely chiselled chin dipping towards the buzz-gun.

And then I speak those words. The words I dread to hear: "I know it's you." My voice is cold, empty.

"Vatic, let me explain. Let me—"

But I don't let her explain. Instead, I press the stud and shoot. A single shot. She crumples over, landing on the dressing table with a crash, the mirror smashing everywhere.

I watch her die, the blood seeping from the hole in her side as big as a melon, my cold, blue eyes glittering back at me from so many broken shards.

"Oh, Vatic…" she gasps.

Those same eyes flick open and the vision leaves me. The woman was… *Esta*. I'm personally responsible for over three million 'quantifiable kills' and only her death affects me. Esta was just another enemy agent, one of many I 'demoted', yet this murder bothers me more than all the rest put together. Her last words: *"Oh, Vatic…"* have haunted me ever since. As to the reason why? The answer is as age old as it is simple.

Because of love.

Because of an emotion I've never been able to feel myself. This is why I was on my way to some colony planet in the backend of nowhere, why I was escaping.

I didn't love Esta. If I'm honest, the only person I have ever loved is myself, although that emotion has of late, been replaced by hate and self-loathing. Love is a difficult sentiment for me. I'm not built for it. I'm neither cold nor unfeeling. If anything, I'm over-sensitive, not that you can tell from my hardened exterior. I merely lack the basic human ability to make such bonds—then again, I'm not properly human. A mutant. I've always been different. An outsider. So why does Esta's death haunt me more than all the others put together? Why does she return to my mind again and again?

I didn't love her, but… Esta loved me.

Esta was also Skilled and unable to love, or so she thought. When she fell, she fell hard and deep. At the time, I didn't care. I used that love to learn her secrets and destroy her. Fate put us on opposite sides of a stupid war and I finished my job with zeal. Vatic, the hero. Vatic, *the Man of Black and White and Blue*. A nickname that once made me so very proud. For that was Vatic—a living symbol of truth and retribution.

Esta's love was to destroy me in the end. Not straightaway. I didn't think of her for years. Not consciously, though I knew she was there. The memory burning inside of me with a cold, terrifying flame. Hundreds of guilty, blue eyes staring back at me from splinters of mirrored glass.

"Oh, Vatic…"

If I could undo one thing in my life, it would be my actions on that day. As that was not a possibility, I simply ran away. I changed my name many times. Moved from planet to planet. I thought myself hidden, safe, yet the Company must've kept tabs on me. I should've been allowed to die in the hold of my colony ship, but the damn Company will never let me go. I'm their war hero, their shining star.

"Vatic, fix me a drink while I'm getting ready."

More memories come flooding back. A cascade. Too many recollections. I push them down—reduce the growing electrical pulses in the memory centres of my brain. And thankfully, they diminish. I concentrate on the now. This moment.

I'm weary, tired. Part of me wants to give up. To let the toxins in my system kill me. But I'm a Skilled. I understand what that means now. It's a curse. I'm compelled to live, to keep living, to find the truth of things. I should've never been in that war, or any war. We, the Skilled, are too driven, too centred—too dangerous. And they lied to us. The damn Company. Made us do things. Terrible things.

Three-million, four-hundred thousand and fifty-eight quantifiable kills.

Yet I know the number is a more than that. A lot more.

I'm a monster.

I'm Vatic, war hero and murderer. The Company put their best man on this job. Me. The angel of death, with the medals to prove it. *Vatic.* That must count for something.

boosted

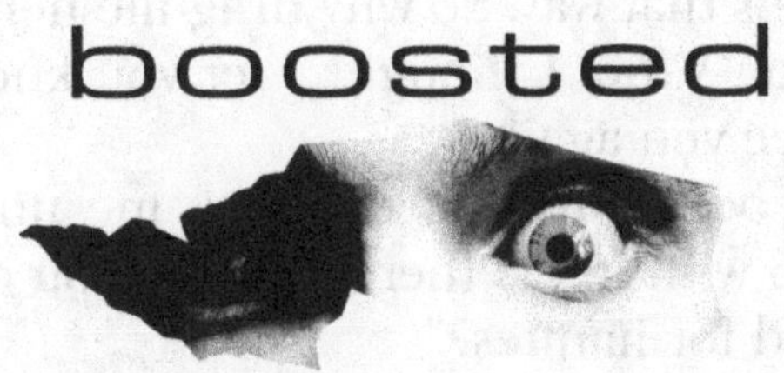

I RAISE myself to unsteady feet and stumble towards Offia's lab. The display on her door says 'Biology Bitch' and despite recent events, the nom-de-plume raises a smile. I hit the chime and she lets me in. Her high forehead furrowing at the sight of me.

"Shit, Vatic! What happened?"

I must look worse than I realise. "Flashbacks and memories is what happened."

"I don't understand." She guides me into her lab—the smallest and most cramped so far—and offers me a sac of water.

I break the membrane with my teeth and swallow. There's no time for explanations. "The results. What did you find?"

Offia shrugs. "There's not much to tell. Everything checks out. The body was very probably Chen's. His DNA profile is a close match to what I would guess is his genetic ancestry—that's from just knowing the man, observing him, so I can't give you a definite ID. The bloods were clean—for anything we know about."

I sigh. "Nothing unusual? Nothing at all?"

A shake of her head.

"Shit!"

"At a dead end, huh?"

"Sure feels that way. So why drag me here?"

"I like you Vatic. I thought I let you know that. I wanted to see you again."

An idea occurs to me, catching me unawares. I decide to go with it. "Is there any way you can check Chen's blood for nanites?"

"Nanites? They haven't used that technology for years. Why?" Realisation dawns across her smooth features. "Trinny Lunn… you suspect her?"

"Just answer the question."

Her lips purse in thought. "I'd have to tweak some of my test equipment—nanites haven't been in vogue for a long time, but yeah, I can do that, if you think it will help."

"Good. Get started straightaway."

"So… you gonna tell me why that stuck-up white bitch is in your sights?"

"To be honest, I'm just clutching at straws, I no more suspect Lunn than I do anyone else."

The furrows reappear on Offia's high forehead. She seems disappointed.

"You wanted her to be involved?"

She smiles guiltily. "I'm not proud to say this—a murder is a lot more interesting than a dumb suicide."

"Well, here's your chance to incriminate somebody." I sit down, hunger gnawing at my insides. A thought occurs to me. "You say Chen's outage ruined your schedule?"

"The man was a bona-fide pest."

"Tell me, what work are you doing here, exactly?"

Offia takes time to answer the question. "Like I said. I was running a complex gene-sequencing programme."

"That's hardly the white-heat of scientific research. More like the everyday bullshit you'd find at any standard medical facility."

Offia reddens and I know I've hit the spot.

"And you call this a lab? The place is a closet, especially compared to Chen's dome. You must've noticed how impressive his laboratory is in comparison to yours?"

"Only a man would come up with such a dumb statement. I don't require much room. Everything I need is right here."

I cast an eye around the cramped lab. Nothing more than an array of gene-sequencers hooked up to a data-centre and a few other non-descript machines and equipment. "Cut the crap, Offia, and tell me what's going on."

Offia sits down on a stool opposite and sighs. "I was really starting to like you." She pinches the skin on her smooth rounded chin with a worried hand. "The Company," she begins and already I'm hating those two words with a vengeance, "put my research on hold, just for a short time, so I could concentrate on this gene-sequencing program."

"When was that?"

"I'll be getting back to my study when all this DNA crap is finished."

"When?"

"Shortly after I arrived... two years ago, give or

take a few months. But this last batch will be over in a couple of weeks and I can get started again."

Does she really believe that? She's been side-lined, like Elbaz. Ackermann has retired himself and Chen was soon for the chop. Even the impressive Trinny Lunn could be just as redundant as the rest. Her subject of nanobiology certainly was.

"And I'm getting a new lab. They promised me."

"So you do have designs on Chen's place, huh?"

A wry smiles appears upon Offia's full lips. "I can't say that hasn't crossed my mind. You think that's a good enough motive for murder?"

"I wish it was. I admit it. I'm stumped. At a dead end."

"I'm glad to finally talk about what's been going on. You don't know what it's been like, having to pretend my work here was on par with those other bastards. Once the sequencers are running, I'm pretty much a spare wheel. I actually enjoyed that blood-work. The most proper science this bitch has done in a long time."

"Then why hide behind such a dumb story?"

"Hey! My research aint dumb, okay?" Every muscle in Offia's frame seemed to tense at once. "And don't you get it? This base is just one big melting pot of egos and paranoia—they'd all go to town on me like they did with Chen if they knew what Offia was really doing."

A beep from my wafer.

"Vatic? Are you there?" A smarmy sounding Anton Frederix. *"Can you come see me, I'd like to discuss something with—"* I switch him off.

"What does he want?"

"To gloat over my progress—or lack of it. He said it was a suicide all along. You all did. Still, I might as well go and see him. I've interviewed everyone now. He could know about some of the things I've found out." I try and stand, but my legs are suddenly jelly, and I nearly fall over.

Offia jumps off her stool and stops me from collapsing. "You okay? You look bloody terrible—even worse than the first time I saw you."

"Nothing you can help with."

"You sure?"

"Like I told you, I've just come out of hypersleep."

"How long ago?"

"Four or so hours."

"You're kidding. The shock to your system would be too great for you to—" She stops in mid-sentence. "...*Not you*. Only a Skilled could survive such a procedure. Space! You must've had a rough ride."

"Tell me about it."

Offia helps me back onto my stool, where I balance precariously. I'm more tired than I realised.

"And what the hell were you doing in hypersleep?" she asks with a quick shake of her head. "That's the cheapest and the dumbest way to travel. You know they deliberately turn off ten percent of the living cargo to get their wastage fee and save costs, don't you?"

"You're not the first person to remind me of that."

"The Company would pay for better, faster transport. Why take the risk?"

"I wasn't working for the Company, not until they

woke me up and dumped me on this damn rock."

She looks me up and down. "You're dying."

"How do you know?"

"Hey, I'm the *Biology Bitch*—one of the best, or so I thought. Until they sent me here. Whoever did this to you must've used some serious enzymes and quite nasty chemicals. You need a full blood scrub."

I scan around her cramped lab. "You possess such a machine?"

A quick shake of her head. "And with no Medic, you're screwed." Her lips squeeze into a tight, supportive smile. "How long have you got?"

I glance down at my wafer:

1 hour, 38 minutes.

"Not long."

"Does anyone else know you're on the clock?"

"No, and I'd like to keep things that way. I need to get going." I slide off my stool, and stumble towards the exit hatch.

"Stop." Offia's voice is quiet, but commanding. "I think I can help you."

I turn to face her. "How?"

"You may only have over an hour to live, but your organs are gonna start shutting down long before then. I can give you something to keep you going. A sort of... um, booster."

"Is it dangerous?"

"Less dangerous than dying."

"What'll it do?"

"Not quite kill you..."

"Great. Will the stuff give me any extra time?"

"I dunno, maybe. It's a sort of stimulant. You okay

with that?”

“I don’t have a choice.”

She disappears for a few minutes, and comes back holding a suspicious-looking hypo-spray. I pull down my skinsuit and Offia presses it to my neck. A brief blast of compressed air and I’m hit with what feels like pure adrenaline. My whole system is jolted into vibrant, buzzing life. All my senses are heightened— the sounds of Offia’s lab magnified, my vision suddenly brighter and full of intensified colour.

“Whoa!” I say, swaying on the stool.

The deep pain in my joints and limbs is blasted away. I’m charged and overcome with an almost religious euphoria. I’ve had something similar before—one of the most popular and illegal recreation stims ever produced. But this is above and beyond anything I’ve ever taken.

“That’s Boost!” I blurt, using the stim’s street name, aware that I’m almost shouting. “Where in space did you get your hands on it? Boost has been off the market for years.”

“Five years ago, to be precise.”

“You mean…?”

Offia bowed. “Guilty as charged. And Boost is one hell of a charger. Not that I use stims myself.”

“You’re a drug-designer? That’s… that’s unbelievable.”

“I suppose I didn’t expect the thing to catch on as well as it did. I work for the Company—they’re not stupid. They would’ve caught on to my little operation sooner or later. I dropped out of the loop long before they raided the production labs. But yeah, it was quite the success story."

I point a trembling finger towards the hypo-spray. "And you refined the formula?"

"I sure did. Good, huh?"

I look at Offia with new eyes. She's a lot more than just a simple scientist—not that scientists are simple—but to be involved in drug manufacture and trafficking? I'm both shocked and impressed.

"How do you feel?"

I pull myself up to my full height, which is still a little shorter than Offia. "Fantastic!"

"Good."

"Although, I'm guessing the comedown is gonna be one long bummer?"

Offia smiles, her teeth flashing at me for a second. "Let's hope you're still around to enjoy it."

"Me too… I'd better go see the Director and put a bit of stick about. Solve this thing."

"You won't say anything regarding my… my lack of real research or my hobby?"

I shake my head. "No, not yet."

"What does that mean?"

"There's other stuff I've found out."

"You gonna tell Offia?"

I shake my head.

"I won't spill the beans if you don't." She offers me her hand.

"I keep schtum about what I've seen in here and you tell no one I'm dying, is that the idea?"

"You sure catch on quick."

There's no way I can promise, though I don't tell her that. I take her hand and shake.

Offia seems reluctant to let me go. "If you need anything more from me, just ask, okay?"

"You still offering me that candy, huh?"

"I've another shot of Boost, we could… share the experience."

"I thought you didn't partake yourself."

"I can make the odd exception."

One thing about Boost is increased brain activity and mental processing. I'm still on the clock. Regardless if I'm stimmed up to the gills, I don't need a super-charged cerebellum to tell me time is running out. "Later, when I've solved this thing, okay."

"You don't have much of a later."

"You want to strike while the iron is hot, is that it?"

"You can't blame me for trying."

I lean over and kiss her on the lips. Nothing more than a quick peck. "Check for those nanites."

Offia reluctantly lets go of my hand. "I'll also attempt to rig up something to help your blood problem. But don't hold your breath. Come back and see me soon, okay?"

I nod. "Soon is all I've got."

moulds

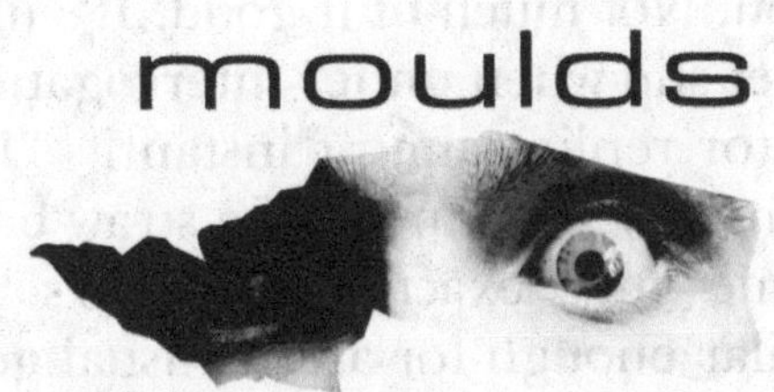

HABITATION IS empty. I was hoping to find Bill, but the canteen is silent.

The door to Frederix's office is open. I stroll in, marvelling at the lack of pain in my joints and muscles. I also feel warm, the deep chill inhabiting my bones has been burned away. Or more accurately, *Boosted away.*

I find the Director sitting behind his enormous desk working at his data-centre. He lifts his head and glances at me with those milky, pale blue eyes of his. They stare for a moment, followed by a tight, forced smile. He doesn't like me—his expression tells me this in no uncertain fashion, despite the grin plastered over his lower face.

I glance at his drinks cabinet. Still empty. "You… needed to see me?"

"Vatic," he says expansively, the drawl of his voice even more exaggerated. "I think we may have gotten off on the wrong foot. I wanted to apologise for earlier. I'm not used to people treading on my toes. I over-stretched my authority."

I ignore his cliché-ridden apology. He's not brought me here to say sorry. It's just another power play. I decide to try to make him squirm. "I've heard a lot about you. Not much of it good. It's interesting what people let slip when under interrogation."

The Director replies almost instantly. "I have no doubt that's the case. I'm more of a straw boss, if you understand me—not exactly everyone's manager, although similar enough for all the usual gossip and dislike that goes with the position. It's water off a duck's back to me."

I hit him with a stare and, in my present state of mind, my eyes feel like twin shining beacons. "From what I hear, you can't keep your dick zipped."

"That's neither here nor there, is it?" he says with an 'I couldn't give a shit' shrug. "My personal life has little or no bearing on Chen's suicide—not unless you think we had a lover's tiff?" A small laugh escapes from his tight lips. "Joking aside, I can categorically confirm my nether regions went nowhere near the man. He was not my type. I like them young. Hence my little contretemps with Bill—I'm assuming that's what you're talking about?"

I say nothing.

"A mistake. Yet, as you may or may not know from your own experience, if one doesn't take chances, how is one to get the rewards?"

I was hoping to embarrass him. Frederix isn't fazed. If anything, he seems to be enjoying himself. This is not the reaction I expected.

The Director readjusts the glasses with a feminine shaped hand. "Now… how about we move past this irrelevant tittle-tattle and concentrate on the business of the moment. Was there anything of interest in Jelinek's laboratory?"

"He's still dead," I blurt, my voice unintentionally loud.

Frederix pauses for a second. He can see I'm stimmed and appears, if anything, a little jealous. "But no evidence this was anything other than a suicide?"

"There's more to it than that, there has to be."

The Director's tight smile makes a reappearance. "Did you find any proof to the contrary, yes or no?" he asks, his voice sweet like a honey-covered knife.

A quick shake of my head. "Offia is looking into something for me. A new line of investigation," I say with fervour.

"That uptight bitch? I'm surprised you got her to even speak to you."

I ignore him. The man is a misogynist at best, although I guess his hatred doesn't stop at women. "She told me you enjoyed informing Chen of the Company's decision. That you assembled everyone else together and presented them with the good news last night."

The Director sits back in his chair giving every impression he finds my continuing line of enquiry quite the most tedious thing he's had to endure in a long time. He makes another steeple out of his fingers. "Yes, I did. I can't see there's any harm in admitting that. And, as there is no need to be anything other than transparent, let me tell you that when I learned of his death... well, I was as happy as a pig in the proverbial."

I try a different tack "Did Chen ever leave the base?"

Frederix looks thoughtful for a moment. "Actually, now I think about it, I'm pretty sure he's never taken a vacation. And besides, the Company doesn't favour extended breaks. The last thing someone does in his position is to take a holiday."

"If he knew he was about to be canned by the company, why not? It'd be his last chance."

"Not Chen. He was a travel-phobe and liked his routine. The man got sweaty every time a cargo pod arrived. I guess he was worried there might be an accident."

"He thought his life was in danger?" I'm scrabbling around for clues and we both know it.

The Director gives me a wearied look. "Some people always worry. It's who they are." His eyes flash over my hyped-up visage. "How they're *wired*. But not you or me, right? Face facts, Vatic. No one cared enough about the bastard to snuff him out."

I shake my head from side to side and clamp my jaw. My eyes narrow and the muscles in what are left of my cheeks, bulge. I've felt like this before—I have a stubborn streak born from belligerence, though most of all, from experience. I'm Vatic. I never let go. I always keep pushing.

Frederix's voice gains in volume. "Chen killed himself and that's that. A done deal. Over and out. So Vatic, you can either shit or get gone—you've sat on the pot long enough."

"Maybe you're right, but it isn't the whole picture. This investigation is only beginning. I won't leave until I find out what's really going on at Karst Base. You hear me?" My voice is full of confidence and threat, although I'm not sure how much is Vatic and how much is the Boost speaking.

The Director remains unfazed. "Have you considered one other possibility?"

"What?"

"That you're overcooking the entire investigation. I don't know why the Company sent in a Skilled for a straightforward suicide. In the scheme of things, Chen is and was unimportant—nothing to write home about. Perhaps they made a simple mistake—which, as far as I can tell—is more than likely. But you're too arrogant to accept the possibility. You Skilled are all the same. Full of your own sense of justice and retribution. Any other investigator would've accepted the simple facts and made his report. Not you, Vatic. You're too goddamn important. So why don't you do everyone a favour and drop this thing and go back to wherever you came from."

Frederix has no idea how much I would like to do just that. "I may hate the Company, but they don't make many mistakes. I'm not irrational. I've considered such a possibility very carefully. Yet my mind keeps returning to the same sticking point. Why go to the trouble of pulling me out of hypersleep? Me. Vatic." I think back to Chen's second chance, to Elbaz's redundant hydroponics lab and to Trinny Lunn's archaic nanites and Ackermann and Offia. To the disabled security system and the missing medic. "Call it arrogance, call it obsession, call it any number of things, but nothing in this investigation adds up.

The Company brought me here for a purpose. And if it's not Chen's suicide, it's gotta be something else."

Frederix continues as if he hasn't heard a word I've said. "You need to get a grip and face facts. I don't have to remind you that there's a lot of top-notch research going on here, work that cannot be interrupted any longer by your misguided obsession, nor by your frankly gung-ho attitude."

"And what top-notch work is that?"

The Director purses his lips with irritation. "You've visited all the labs I take it? Met everyone. Discussed their relationship with the dead man and their research? You've crossed the T's and dotted the I's?"

I nod, wondering where he's going with this.

"Well then you know first-hand just how vital their combined disciplines are to the Company."

It seems Frederix has no idea what's happening here. Or at least is trying to give me that impression. I find him difficult to read—like the others. It frustrates me. It's as if I'm stumbling around in the dark. I decide to change tack again. "Why is there no Medic on the base?"

The Director's answer is a single, bemused-sounding "What?"

"It's a simple question."

He sits back heavily in his faux-leather chair. "Every base has a Medic as part of standard procedure. Ours was recalled and no replacement was ever sent."

"You never queried that?"

"You don't query the Company, Vatic," he says, as if to do so would court ruin and abandonment. "But

I wasn't totally idle. At first, I thought it an oversight. I made a request for a replacement, and was told one would be made available as soon as they found the right person."

"How long ago?"

"Two years."

"That's quite some recruitment procedure. Don't tell me that's not odd."

"A little unusual," he admits begrudgingly.

I decide to push him a little further to see how he reacts. "Do you want to know what I think?"

"Not really, yet I get the feeling you're going to tell me anyway."

"I think it's a little too convenient that the security system is off-line, don't you?"

"As I said before, it was fixed after the first outage, although subsequent interruptions in the power supply meant maintenance became problematic. But again," he sighs dramatically, "I've not been idle. As I've already told you, I made many requests for an update, to protect the system against further power problems, yet we're dealing with secretive scientists, some with a lot of influence. They all think I spend my time listening in on them as it is, or that the others are somehow hacking the system to steal their work. It's not such an unusual paranoia in such successful people. It's possible one of them is blocking the upgrade."

From what I've seen of the so-called scientists so far, this explanation seems implausible, yet Frederix gives every impression of believing this is the case. I decide to go with it, to see what he has to say. "Any idea who that might be?"

His steeple of fingers collapses into a conjoined fist, his two thumbs coming to rest under his chin. "We have some of the best brains here—it could be any one of them."

I've got nowhere with this investigation. A dead end. I'm full of energy with no way to use it. I stand up and try my last avenue of investigation. "One other thing. The underwear I found in your rooms… where did it come from?"

"You're back to that are you?"

"Just answer the damn question."

Frederix's voice is a sneer. "Not from Offia or that tight-assed Trinny Lunn. That's for sure. You were well off the mark there. Call it a trophy."

"Huh?"

"Someone special who I… *bagged*. Just a keepsake. You've found out the kind of man I am. It's hardly an admission."

A name pops into my mind. *"Irenka?"*

For the first time since I entered his office, Frederix seems taken aback. His hands part, the fingers absentmindedly drumming on his desk. His eyes leave mine for a second and disappear into the mid-distance. "Yes," he says quietly. "Yes, it was. She was the intern before Bill. We had a good thing for a time, but she suddenly took a placement elsewhere. Her career, you know. More important than matters of the genitals."

I push him further. "Where did she go to?"

The conjoined hand appears again, his fingers interlocked, his thumbs tapping together. "I never checked. I was upset. Angry. She left quickly."

"Find out," I say. "I want to have a chat with her."

Frederix smiles. "Sure. I'll put it at the top of my list of pointless things to do. Now, are we done?"

"Not quite. Your lab. It's about time I took a looksee."

"I can assure you my research dome contains nothing of interest."

"I'll be the judge of that."

"You know I'm an Exo-biologist?"

I nod.

"It's one of those fields that gets everyone over-excited. Alien life-forms and all that extra-terrestrial life nonsense is great for fiction and entertainment, yet the reality is far different, believe me." Frederix's voice, if possible, becomes more pompous. "Early in my career, when God was still a kid…"

He flicks his eyes at me in comical fashion and I guess he's prepared this little speech.

"…my star was very bright indeed. I was one of the best extra-terrestrial specialists in my field. Some quite valuable medicines were developed from the alien lichen and mould that formed the basis of my study. But success is a journey not a destination, Mr Vatic. Something you may wish to consider. When I came here, I arrived as Director. My investigations continued as a hobby only. A sacrifice I was more than willing to pay… for the greater good of the Company."

"Lichen and mould?" Knowing the man, I expected something far showier.

"You're not impressed?" he shrugs. "To the layman, my research may seem mundane. In the scientific world? Well, what can I say other than it shone as a beacon of light where all around was shadow and darkness."

I'm not sure I believe him and decide to use a cliché of my own. "So why give it all up, why come here as Director and play co-pilot to these jumped-up egos?"

"I'm no co-pilot," he blurts. "I run this base, Vatic. Not them."

"That's no answer."

"Let's just say I fancied a change and leave it there."

"But your work continues as a hobby?"

"I'll let you find out for yourself."

The way he phrases the words seems like he's daring me to find something, or he's purposely misleading me. "More moulds?" I say with a sneer.

"Yes, that's about the measure of it. If you want to give them the once-over, I'm not going to stand in your way."

"You're not coming with me?"

"Let's say I've spent too much time in your company already. Besides, I have to locate Irenka for your… little chat. A lot more interesting than wandering around my old lab and talking to you."

interns

I EXIT the Director's quarters and nearly bump into Bill.

"Hi Vatic," he says glancing at my face with a frown. "You look… um… different."

"I've perked up."

"You sure have…"

It's obvious he wants to ask about the reason behind the change in my demeanour, yet he controls himself. I'm glad he doesn't push it. Stuffing myself with stims is not that bad a thing, particularly as it's helping me to keep going, but I dunno, I want Bill to think well of me. As to why? I have no idea. My reputation has never bothered me before, although I've always had an affinity with the young. Maybe it's because their minds are not as polluted as those who, by the very nature of living a full life, are older, wiser and… darker.

"You been chatting to the Director again?"

I nod.

"How was he?"

"Pissed off."

A smile creeps across Bill's boyish face.

We share a laugh. "Offia told me Frederix is one whole lotta creep." I decide not to mention exactly what she said.

The kid blushes. "Yeah… yeah he is. You don't know the half of it. But it's no longer a problem. If everything goes to plan, I'm getting out of here soon."

"You are?"

"Don't tell anyone, especially the Director, but I've got a new position… on Earth."

"Earth. Wow. How did you wangle that?"

"Lucky, I suppose."

"Quite some career advancement."

"I'm just finalising my transfer—it's not a done deal, but you know the Company. Even Earth needs guys like me to sweep up and make the coffee!"

We both laugh again, yet I sense the move is a significant promotion. A thought occurs to me. "Back in Chen's quarters you said you knew your way around a data-centre. Your speciality. Apart from being a qualified omelette specialist and spacewalker, what did you major in?"

The question throws Bill for a second. "Pure Processing," he says.

"I've never heard of that particular field."

"A new area of research. Think of computing plus, plus, plus—and then add some."

"Are you aware the security system is on the blink?"

"I wouldn't know either way. I'm an intern. I don't even have clearance to go take a shit outside my quarters."

"The Director believes Chen's experiments

knocked the cameras out. And that the system's not been on for a few months—or someone here hacked a way in. Would that be possible?"

"The Company algorithms are pretty unbreakable. They have to be with all the hysteria surrounding espionage. It'd take either a brain bigger than anyone on this base to break the codes or someone with access to serious computing power."

"Sounds to me like you're talking about Trinny Lunn."

Bill unconsciously stiffens.

"You have history with her?" I ask all coy. I know I can trust Bill. He saved my life, but Trinny is a different matter.

He shakes his head vehemently. Too vehemently. I decide not to push the matter. For a seventy-something, Trinny has not yet lost her charms. Hell, I even kissed her, although I'm not gonna lay that onto the kid. I wouldn't blame him if he's secretly knocking her off. His job here seems low on perks. "Could Trinny hack the security system?"

A shrug. "The way code-systems work is simple. Any half-decent computer can crack any cypher the Company uses. Yet the process takes time. Anything up to a couple of weeks. And here's the trick: the algorithms change over a billion times every hour. It'd take a more than a genius to break the system."

This is not the answer I want to hear. "There's no way in?"

"I'd like to help," says Bill. "But with biometric locking, admittance is only for those with rights. To get entry to a locked system, Director Frederix would have to be present in person. With no one in close proximity. He also wouldn't have the power to grant rights to anyone else."

"So I couldn't have seen the security footage if I wanted to?"

"Unless the Company granted you the same access, the answer is no."

"Shit!"

"What is it?"

I take out my wafer and tap it into life. "Maybe the Company did just that." I flick through the screens, my mind taking in the countdown with a stab of worry:

1 hour, 8 minutes.

Time is running out and already I can feel the effects of the stim wearing off.

I navigate the menus with ease and arrive at three flashing words 'SECURITY SYSTEM CLEARANCE'. "You know the saying, Bill?"

The kid looks at me, following my every word like a puppy dog. "Huh?"

"The two most common elements in the universe are hydrogen and stupidity. Seems like I've an inexhaustible supply. I'll let you guess which one it is."

"You've already got access?"

I nod, tapping through a few security screens. "I'm gonna need a data-centre to make this work. I want to do this without Frederix or anyone else knowing. Your rooms?"

Bill seems taken aback.

"Unless you've got something to hide."

"No, it's just that… sure. Come with me."

I follow him to the hatchway and we enter another identical set of living quarters to that of the Director and Chen.

The scene that meets me is not what I expected. His rooms are functional and tidy. The sofa, dull red and knocked out of shape, has seen better days, although it looks comfortable and well used. There are few accoutrements. A beat-up electric guitar, a rack for hanging various sneakers, a dartboard and nothing else. No photographs of friends or family. No digivids of famous singers or sport stars.

Only his data-centre is messy. Papers and wafers litter all the free surfaces around the console.

Maybe I anticipated something a bit more youthful. Then again, Bill is not a typical twenty-something. He's most probably an egghead—he'd have to be a mega-brain to even be here. And, despite his self-effacing comments, working on Earth was a massive step upwards in his career.

The kid is uneasy at my presence. His relaxed demeanour replaced with something more awkward.

"You alright?"

He stares at me with his pleasingly brown eyes, the side of his mouth twisting into a wry smile. "Just a little freaked out."

My war hero history flashes into my mind. "You should be."

"What do you mean?"

I dismiss his question with a quick shake of my head. "Get your data-centre started and give me guest access. I can do the rest."

Bill goes over to a functional desk. He casually

collects his papers and slides them into a folder, stacking his wafers into a neat pile and putting them on a high shelf. He's trying to be nonchalant, yet he's hiding something.

"What's with all that stuff?"

"Just some research I'm working on. My career."

"Secret?"

Bill looks uncomfortable. I've put him on the spot.

He furrows his eyebrows and a pained expression creases his smooth features. "Not that I don't trust you, but—"

"S'okay. I get it."

Bill activates his data-centre with a few waves of his hand and indicates for me to sit down. I place my wafer next to the display and… I'm in. The screen fills with over fifty blank rectangles.

"Huh?" says Bill over my shoulder.

"Seems like the Director was telling the truth. I scroll back in time. Days, weeks, months. Just black static. No recording. Nothing.

"Bad news?"

"I was kinda banking on this footage showing me something I didn't know."

"Like Chen's murderer?"

I nod—a quick stab of my head.

"So you still think he was killed?"

"I don't know what to think."

"That bad, huh?"

"Yeah. Everything is pointing towards this whole thing being a bug hunt."

"You're still wondering why you were brought in for a simple suicide?"

"Too many things are simply not adding up."

Bill lowers his voice. "Can you tell me?"

I want to mention how the much-vaunted Zeta-Karst Laboratories seem to be full of losers, creeps and fakes. Instead, I keep my lip buttoned. I'm no blabbermouth. "Best I don't. I've trod on enough egos in the last couple of hours."

"Yeah, you're probably right... Is there anything you want? I'm the gopher around here. You still look famished. Can I get you something more to eat? Or maybe a drink?"

The Boost has hit me so hard that I'm not sure if I'm hungry or not. "You got any whisky?"

Bill shrugs me an 'I wish' and smiles apologetically.

"Before I go, there is one thing you can help me with."

The kid nods enthusiastically. "Sure."

"Tell me about Irenka."

"Irenka... but she left months ago."

"Let's just say something about her is niggling me."

"You sure are thorough... what do you want to know?"

"Anything would be useful."

"She was the intern when I arrived. As usual, there was a two-week handover period."

"And you two... got it on, yes?"

Bill nods, a smile breaking out over his face. "How'd you know?"

"Apparently I have a talent for these kind of things. It was the way you talked about her back at the airlock."

"I can see I'll have to watch myself around you."

"Was Irenka friendly with anyone else?"

"What are you suggesting?"

I tilt my head and raise my eyebrows at the kid. "Make a guess."

"She wasn't seeing anyone. She made a point of telling me that. One of the problems of being an intern is that everyone sort of expects us to… *well, you know.*"

"Did she mention any one person trying it on?"

"From my own experience, that was probably everybody. Except Elbaz. He keeps to himself. But the rest? Yeah. All of them."

"Was she… interested?"

"Hell no! But she took pity on me. Told me I was her one-week thing. And…"

"Go on."

"Well, she acted like it had been a while for her, if you know what I mean…"

The kid blushes and in that moment I see inside of him. I get a flash of his feelings. Pride, excitement, and a little nervousness. I read him easily. "She never went with the Director?"

Bill makes the obvious connection. "Those clothes you found in the Director's rooms? You think they were Irenka's?"

"That's what Frederix told me. He said they were quite an item. From what I can tell, her leaving Zeta-Karst affected him badly."

He shakes his head. "No way. She despised him. If I hadn't arrived early to replace her, she was going to leave anyway—because of Frederix."

That sounds consistent with what I know of the man, yet I didn't get any sense Frederix was lying to me about the previous intern. "Thanks Bill," I say. "You're a good kid. Can you point me in the direction of Frederix's lab?"

"He's letting you in there?"

"He doesn't have a choice."

"You know what, Vatic?" he says, patting me on my shoulder. "You can come stay with me anytime you want and I'll make sure there's plenty of whisky for you."

ghosts

FREDERIX'S LAB, like all the others, is located on the outer corridor ringing Habitation. I enter the boxlike hub section. The display says 'Director'. And the use of that simple word sums up the man perfectly. Arrogant. Self-important and grandiose.

I'm not expecting to discover anything of importance inside, yet I feel the need to be thorough, particularly as the man is a pompous ass of the highest order. And besides, I'm sure he was daring me to find something. Otherwise my investigation has pretty much stalled. Other than ransacking everyone's personal rooms, which I might be forced into, there's nothing left for me to investigate.

I go to the eye scanner. A brief flash of gentle light illuminates the back of my eye and, for a moment, I glimpse a spaghetti of arteries and veins—the reflection of my retina. I hear the click and whir of the hatches unlocking, the magnetic clamps depolarising. And immediately something feels amiss. Red lights flash across my cerebral cortex in warning. I jerk my head away as a needle jabs out, catching me a glancing scratch against my eye-socket and half of my vision winks out.

Poison!

A neurotoxin of some kind racing down the nerves, crashing into my synapses. I feel the contaminant as a nest of black, writhing vipers—trying to escape. Trying to force their way into my system. I shut down the blood supply to the skin and arteries in my right eye. Closing off the whole area. I know the risk—starved of oxygen those tissues may soon die, yet I have no other option. It's pure force of will, but I manage to keep the poison at bay. My reaction time was almost instantaneous, within milliseconds. Something I couldn't have done without Offia's stim, without Boost.

I stumble into the Director's laboratory. The dome is lit in strange hues, darker than outside and stuffed with twenty to thirty glass tanks. With my one good eye, I look around for a receptacle, a dish, bowl or a cup. I see a stack of petri-dishes by a workstation. I grab at them, knocking them over with a crash. I catch one and I position the plastic saucer under my injured eye, focussing on the poison, guiding it, capillary, by capillary, to my tear duct.

Sudden searing pain. I shut down the nerves and force the toxin out as a single teardrop that trickles into the dish.

I open what I'm hoping is a fridge and find a water sac, slapping the container into my face and rinsing the remaining poison from my skin.

I go back to the hatchway and squint at the eye-scanner. A needle pokes out, as thin as a strand of hair. A deliberate attack. I realise just how lucky I've been—although luck had nothing to do with it. I'm starting to understand what it's like to be one of the Skilled. Of what that term means. If I could only deal with the hypersleep toxins as I did the neuro-poison, but despite the Boost, time is running out.

On the upside, someone tried to kill me. It sounds stupid, but I'm elated. I knew there was more to this than suicide and this is the proof. I quickly hurry through the cramped corridors to Offia's lab. I hit the chime and she lets me in.

"Your eye," she says, a startled look on her face. "It's swollen. You been in a punch-up with Frederix?"

"I wish. No, this is much better."

"What do you mean?"

"An attempt on my life."

"And that's good news?"

I hold up the petri-dish like a prize. "I'm not dead, and we have this."

"Who did it?"

"Dunno. Booby-trap. They used some kind of neurotoxin. Who does that sound like to you?"

Offia's eyes flick towards the plastic dish with alarm. "Neurotoxin? In a facility like this it could be made by anyone."

"Your best bet?"

"As far as I'm concerned, they're all jumped up, self-important but very capable bastards. I don't see any one of them as a murderer."

"Well someone is."

Offia looks at me with confusion. "You sure it was a neurotoxin?"

I nod.

"And you're okay?"

"I managed to flush the poison out of my system."

"Into the petri-dish?"

"Yep."

"I know the Skilled have control over their autonomic systems, but, shit, that's pretty damn impressive."

"I'm an impressive kinda guy."

"Are you sure you got all the contaminant? Neurotoxins can have a delayed effect. How do your limbs feel? Any numbness?"

I shake my head. "I shut everything down in time."

"How did this happen?"

"The security system outside Frederix's lab. Sabotaged."

"The right side of your face is still pretty swollen."

I concentrate on the affected area, reducing the fluids until I feel the inflammation diminish.

A startled look passes across Offia's features. "That's quite some trick."

"Apparently."

"Did you say *Frederix's lab?*"

"Yeah, whoever it was knew I would be visiting there sooner or later and planted a little surprise for me."

"Are you sure you were the intended victim?"

"You mean the attack could have been meant for the Director?" I consider the possibility. "No one likes the jumped up git and, if there is a killer out there, he'd certainly be a target. Either way, this investigation has taken a turn for the better."

"You're pleased?"

"It means Chen Jelinek was very probably murdered. And the murderer is either after Frederix or worried I'm going to find out their identity. That's gotta be good."

"Here."

She gives me a towel and I hand her the petri-dish containing my single tear before drying myself off. She places it in a small receptacle inside an impressive looking machine and presses a few buttons. The apparatus emits a UV light and hums. She walks to her desk and activates the data-centre.

I go over and stand on her shoulder—a base invasion of another's privacy. Offia doesn't react. It's not exactly intimacy, yet it reveals a level of faith in me that both warms and worries. No one should trust Vatic. No one. They don't know what I'm truly capable of. After everything I've learned today, I frighten even me. "You got a cigarette?" I ask.

"Sure. Although you may want to avoid getting smoke in your eye."

I laugh politely.

She lights two cigarettes taken from a packet sitting on her desk, and passes me one. The other she places between her lips with practiced ease.

The screen flickers into life. A few hand movements and a close-up of my single tear appears. More waved gestures and the view zooms into the molecular level. Onscreen information flashes up in a steady stream.

I drag on the cigarette, blowing the smoke out in one long exhalation. "You see anything?" I say, watching the incomprehensible numbers and letters flicker past with my one good eye.

She sucks on the cigarette in the corner crease of her mouth. "You were right. Neurotoxin. Complex. This little bastard inhibits neuron control over the ion concentrations across cell membranes. It can also interfere and interrupt the communications between nerve synapses."

"Cut the mumbo-jumbo. Tell me, will I see again?"

Offia hesitates.

"I asked you a question."

"You heard of the cyclops?"

"Ouch."

"Full vision is possible again, but the procedure will involve new nerves or a transplant.

"I'm not getting any better?"

"Not without medical help." Offia shakes her head, ash dropping from the end of her cigarette and onto her Jacket. If this bothers her, she doesn't let it show. More information appears on her screen. "You're lucky you only lost an eye. This is nasty. Bio-engineered. If any of the toxin had reached your cerebellum… you would've died instantly. Total brain dysfunction. This girl's not seen anything quite like it before."

"What do you mean… *bio-engineered?*"

Offia rescues the cigarette from her mouth—the end wet with saliva and a trace of lipstick—and flicks the remaining ash into a stub-filled ashtray. "Whoever created this, based the compound on organic tissue."

"A flower?"

Offia turns away from her screen and looks up at me, a smile raising her cheekbones and widening her already large eyes. Her face is bathed in light and curls of enticing smoke. "The sample is full of plant cells… or at least bits of them. How did you know?"

"A hunch," I say, squinting back at her with my one good eye. It's a moment. Intimate. I rest my hand on her head and stroke at her short wiry hair.

She nuzzles against me. A simple gesture that warms me. I like Offia. I didn't expect to. She's certainly not my type—whatever that is—although there is something familiar about her that I can't quite put my finger on. An internal quality. The moment passes. I turn back to her screen and drop my hand. The cigarette finds my lips again, another drag.

"You think Elbaz did this?" she says quietly.

"He's a prime candidate."

"I suppose he is. Hassan has his hydroponic domes, yet these cells could be cultivated in any number of ways. If you're looking for the most likely suspect, look no further than me."

"You're forgetting one thing," I say. "You know I'm already dying. It'd be silly to take the risk of trying to kill me when all you had to do was wait till I either died or was transferred off this rock."

"You're lucky it's not me." Offia tilts her head. "If this bitch designed a poison, you wouldn't be standing here, Skilled or not. Which is a shame as I'm sure you'd wash up a treat—well, once you'd got a few meals in you and maybe worked out a bit and had a shave."

"My height's not a problem then, huh?"

"We both know it's what's between the eyes that matters the most. Well, in your case, next to it."

Offia is a stand-up girl, that's much for sure. "So who's next on the Biology Bitch's toxin hit-list?"

"Frederix, I suppose. He's a biologist as well. Even if his specialty was in exo-studies. Otherwise, it's anyone's guess."

The screen flashes red again and a Latin name appears—*Dendrophylax Lindenii*. Offia's eyebrows lift, before settling back around the bridge of her nose with a gentle furrow. "That's interesting."

"What is?"

"The toxin came from some type of hybrid plant. An orchid that is less of a flower and more like a fungus. The organism is called the *Ghost Orchid*," she says, reading directly from the screen, her cigarette firmly planted in the corner of her mouth again. "Found in beech, oak, pine and spruce forests growing on base-rich soils back on Earth. Not that there's any of them left. The class is long-extinct. Like most species on that worn out rock," she snorted.

I remember the bizarre black flowers growing in Elbaz's Woodland glade. "Can you show me a digivid of the orchid?"

Offia waves her hands and the data-centre screen fills with an image of a flower made up of delicate golds and whites. Little figures in white, almost floating—like ghosts.

"I've seen this flower before."

Offia is startled. "You have? Where?"

"Not exactly like this. They kinda freaked me out. The flowers were bigger, fleshier and black. A whole glade of them back in Elbaz's evergreen forest. That can't be a coincidence. I think I need to pay him another visit."

"I'd be careful, if he's your attempted murderer, walking back into his territory isn't the best idea I've heard of."

She's right. From what I've seen of the man, he's controlled and calculating. If he's my attacker, I wonder why he didn't make an attempt when I visited him. Christ, he could've poisoned me with his rollups, or any number of other ways. The man was wound up, yet I received the sense that I wasn't what he expected. After he found out I had no intention of shutting him down, the fight went out of him. It doesn't add up.

"Okay," I say. "Going back to see Elbaz is a risk too far. Best to round everyone up in the canteen again and thrash this out once and for all. I'll go tell the Director the good news. First, I'll search his laboratory. The location of the attack may have been random, but I want to find out if that booby trap was hiding something."

"Intuition, huh?"

"What's left of it."

"Is there anything else Offia can do?"

"How are you getting on with testing Chen's blood for nanites?" Since the attempt on my life, this seems even more like a blind alley, but I'm not ready to dump my previous intuition.

"I'm doing a full plasma breakdown, taking the whole shebang apart at the molecular level. I've stopped everything else—including all the gene sequencing. The Company has messed me around enough. And besides, Offia is now working on your orders, right?" She seems almost proud.

"How long will the process take?"

"A broad-spectrum test? Maybe forty minutes to an hour, unless you have a sample."

I shake my head. "Keep at it and contact me on the wafer when you get the results." I place a hand on her shoulder. Offia strokes it with delicate fingers.

"Be careful, Vatic."

I stub out my cigarette in her ashtray. "Sure," I say, and stride towards the hatch.

breach

A SHORT while later, I'm again standing outside Frederix's lab. The hatch is open—did I close it when I left? I can't remember.

I examine the needle sticking out of the eye-scanner. A drop of deadly neurotoxin glistens on the tip. Whoever tried to kill me has not returned to clear up their work. I push the hatch open and enter.

The chamber is as I remembered. Just another dome. To be honest, I'm getting sick of the base with its suffocating corridors, mostly identical segments and living areas. The circular space is half-lit and depressing.

I wonder if searching Frederix's lab is a good use of my remaining time, but my gut, or rather my genetically engineered intuition, knows differently.

I wander in the gloom. With one side of my vision missing, I feel vulnerable. Anyone could sneak up on me and I'd be none the wiser. I'm broken. Compromised.

The dome consists of a series of glass-walled, oblong chambers arranged in precise lines, each containing unremarkable rocks covered in even more unremarkable mould—like a high school biology lab, and exactly what Frederix described to me. Maybe he takes me for a sap? In my present state, I'm just that. I've not been myself since I started this damn job.

I put my face next to one of the tanks. The glass compartment contains a single rock, draped over with something that looks like a half-rotted leaf. An actual alien.

I'm not surprised. The idea of extra-terrestrial life has excited humans for generations, although, Earth, it turned out, was pretty much unique. The maths said otherwise, that given the number of galaxies, solar systems and planetary bodies, other Earth-like planets must exist. The problem? No such planets have ever been found.

The Colonies are lifeless rocks—worlds with acceptable gravity at the right distance from their sun or suns, with molten iron cores giving protection from cosmic rays and the ability to hold on to their poisonous atmospheres. Industrial grinders the size of small cities had prepared vast areas of soil-like 'farming land'. Genetically engineered plants spewed oxygen and added nutrients, but it'd be hundreds of years before these planets were anything like Earth. Farming wasn't pleasant. Many generations would pass before the air became breathable without a mask.

If I don't work out this puzzle soon, even that existence will be denied me.

I sit down on a stool and cast my limited gaze around the static lab. Another dead-end. My intuition has let me down. I shrug, wondering why I put so much faith in my insight—or lack of it. This is a waste of time. I need to get Frederix and the others back to the canteen and finish this damn thing. Except…

…I don't move.

I stay where I am, my focus moving to the floor. It's constructed from the same raw materials as the rest of Karst. Printed from the resources found on this asteroid. Commonplace. And yet, it takes all my attention. I tilt my head and spot almost invisible curving grooves. Nothing more than fine lines indicating movement. Someone has dragged a tank aside. Not once but many times. A secret exit or entrance?

I jump off my seat to investigate and nearly fall over.

KLAXONS!

The alarm system blares into life with ear-piercing wails and flashing red lights. A depressurisation alert.

"What the hell!" I shout, racing to the hatchway before it closes automatically.

I emerge into the corridor, the door clanging shut behind me, my fingers tapping the wafer into life. One whole section of the base glows red—Elbaz's domes. Somehow, I intuitively knew it would be Hassan Elbaz.

I sprint towards his laboratory, expecting to see some of the others. But I'm alone. I hit Elbaz's chime and check my handheld again. With only one eye, it's difficult to focus. Through the blurs, the wafer blinks: *'OUTER HULL BREACH'*. All five domes are still flashing red, which means venting atmosphere.

They can't all have been compromised.

At the first sign of decompression, automatic

protocols ensure doors and hatchways close themselves, isolating the leak to just one area—either they'd failed, or something serious had happened. Another glance at the wafer tells me the base is in lock-down. I countermand the automatic procedure and almost immediately Frederix's voice shouts at me.

"What in the name of the Company do you think you're doing?"

"None of your concern. Elbaz's lab has been breached. We can't leave him in there."

"Don't be stupid! You'll put everyone at risk, you'll—"

I switch Frederix off. He needn't have worried. Elbaz's hatch won't open. Even when I send the emergency over-ride. "Shit!"

I try again. Nothing.

"I'm going to try and get in to the depressurised area from outside," I broadcast over the com.

Only Offia replies. *"Be careful, Vatic."*

"In the meantime, get Bill and see if you can find a way through Elbaz's hatch."

I run around the curve of the corridor, opening doors as I go, and dart into the service tunnel leading to the Auxiliary Hub. The bug is still parked and ready to go in its mini-airlock. I jump into the pilot's seat and punch the start button on the pristine dash.

Airtight hatch doors shut behind me and the transport is now independent of Karst Base, its balloon-like tyres resting on a raised runway leading towards a landing pad.

If I keep the bug close to the buildings, I should be able to find enough artificial gravity to glue this thing to the ground. I hit the control stick and the six-wheeler rolls off the runway and onto the dust-covered surface. The vehicle immediately bucks forward, tipping with its own momentum and suddenly I'm a passenger. The out-of-control buggy tumbles over and bounces, once, twice, three times before coming to rest on its side. My depth vision is shot to pieces, I realise as I unconsciously rub at my useless eye, cursing my own stupidity and bad luck. But I won't give up. I'm Vatic. I never give up.

In the asteroid's meagre gravity, the transport weighs no more than a helium-filled balloon, or at least that's what it feels like. I slowly start to rock the chassis until I can feel it tipping over. I put all of my reduced weight in the command seat and lean into the dash. The bug rights itself, although I'm still too far away from the base's artificial gravity field. I've no choice but to use the control lever again. And this time I'm not as heavy-handed. A slight push and the vehicle lurches forwards leaving the surface for a few seconds before, landing on its fattened wheels. Another nudge and I'm half-rolling, half-bouncing towards Elbaz's domes.

Suddenly the gravity returns and I fall into the seat with a jolt, my remaining breath knocked out of me. I manoeuvre in close, following the vast curve of the closest hemisphere. So far, no damage. Maybe the breach is a false alarm? A way to get me outside the base—although my present actions were difficult to premeditate. From what I've found out about myself, I'm a man of action, not considered deliberation.

A buzz on the dash. Frederix again. *"Bring the bug*

back to the dock and that's an order!" His voice has lost all control. He's furious.

"You think you can stop me?"

"There are strict decompression guidelines, Vatic. We sit tight and wait for the auto-repair systems to do their job. Company protocol. Get back here, now."

If there's one character-trait shared by myself and Frederix, it's stubbornness. "I'm starting to wonder if you have really understood the whole 'who's in charge thing'?"

"You're endangering yourself and the entire base!"

I glance at the wafer. Elbaz's domes are still glowing red. "Looks like auto-repair is malfunctioning. Who would've guessed?"

"Let me assure you that I will be writing a stern report to the Company about this incident."

"Go screw yourself!" I mute the intercom.

I round a second vast hemisphere and brake the bug to a sliding stop. Sand and freeze-dried plant life, erupting like a sideways volcano, billow from a breach in the dome's side large enough to drive the transport into. This is both good and bad. Good, because there's still air in the dome, bad, because if I try and get the six-wheeler through the rent, the thing is likely to be blown into space. Me with it.

I push the lever forward and arrive at the gap just as a frozen lizard spirals past the bug's window. Elbaz's desert dome.

Not anymore.

How the hell am I going to get inside? I take a quick look at the dash—and notice an emergency control panel. I flick open the board to reveal an array of switches and levers.

Grappling hooks!

I shake my head. Of course! With such low gravity, the transport was fitted with a set of harpoons to help anchor the machine to the surface in emergencies.

I reverse out of the artificial grav and fire the first missile into the belching gap. The force of the launch throws the compact backwards, but the line holds. I let off two more harpoons and start to winch myself in. The wake from the escaping air blows the six-wheeler aloft, buffeting it left and right but, gradually, with a few worrying scrapes and groans, the vehicle is pulled through the breach. The gravity returns a second later. The bug falls with a thump and I'm bounced out of my seat.

I'm in Hassan's desert area—what's left of it— nothing more than a whirling sandstorm of foliage and other detritus from Elbaz's vast experimental domes. Grit and frozen sand crack against the windscreen.

I need to find the hatchway leading to the inner dome and fast. I detach the winches and the bug drifts backwards, the cold vacuum of space trying to suck the compact back out onto the surface of the asteroid. I hit the accelerator hard. The six-wheeler slides left and right, but is going nowhere.

I have four harpoons remaining. I fire two directly ahead, both plunging into the pseudo-desert floor. I release the brakes and wind myself forward whilst simultaneously gunning the engine. The electrics whine in complaint—it's do or die. After a few moments, I'm out of the worst of the turbulence and worming my way along the inner wall.

I haven't gone far, when I spot a hatchway belching a sea of green. Elbaz's tropical dome—not where I want to be heading, yet I don't have a choice. Ripped plastic sheeting flaps crazily in the maelstrom. The pressurisation doors are open. They should've closed automatically as soon as the rupture occurred. This is wrong with a capital: 'What the fuck is going on?'

I manoeuvre the bug as close to the exit as I can—without the wind blowing me away—and launch the remaining two harpoons into the wall either side of the opening. I gun the engine again and wind in both winches. The bug lurches forward, gathering quite some speed, hits a series of rocks and flies through the air. I sit back in the command seat, secure the safety belt and brace myself for impact. Sudden deceleration as the out-of-control machine crashes into the corridor, shearing off antennae and wheels. The transport crumples around me, but I'm protected by an emergency burst of anti-grav. The window smashes. Red lights flash on the dash and alarms go off. I cannot hear them above the scream of escaping air and exploding tyres. Already I'm shutting down my breathing and diverting blood to my major organs and muscles.

I clamber through the smashed windscreen, whipped by wind, vegetation and mud. A heavy branch catches me a glancing blow on my forehead, knocking me to the ground. A fortuitous accident—the crown of an immense tree flies into the corridor, its outer branches shorn off by the narrow tunnel, and hits the crumpled bug with an almighty bang—

just missing me. Plants, soil and other detritus follow it into the tight passageway, pelting and whipping at me until the screaming wind suddenly stops.

The bug has blocked the corridor connecting the desert and jungle areas—but it's a temporary stopper at best. I lurch to my feet, climbing amongst a maze of smashed tree trunks and crushed vegetation to emerge through ripped, plastic curtains into what must've been Hassan's jungle dome. The place is immense, and the damage catastrophic. Trees torn up by the roots—mud and soil everywhere. And birds, hundreds of them, dead amongst the detritus as well as other animals I don't recognise.

A quick glance at my wafer tells me the direction of the central dome. I take an exploratory breath. There is still oxygen in the air, but not much. Enough for someone like me to survive. Behind me, the whistling of escaping air starts around the bug and increases in volume. I locate the door mechanism, hoping to seal the passageway from this end. It's sturdy enough to have resisted the bombardment and the hydraulics should have enough power to crush anything trapped in between. The control panel flashes with amber light. I hit the close button. Nothing. I try again. More nothing. Redundancy is built into all systems. The Company might not care much for life, but they make up for that when it comes to protecting their installations. It leads to one conclusion—sabotage.

I pull back an emergency panel in the wall and fold out a lever. I turn the handle, one revolution, two, and the doors begin to move. I won't be able to shut them fully, but narrowing the gap can only help.

I dig deep for energy reserves I don't have. Releasing glucose into my system from wherever I can find it and crank the mechanism further. Another few inches. I hear the bug creaking as the vacuum, from what must be nearly airless space behind, pulls upon it.

The gap between both doors is down to just a couple of feet when the negative pressure inside the desert dome finally sucks the smashed buggy out of the corridor. Wind screams in a wailing gale and I dive away, rolling. A vast tree, wrenched from the ground, hurtles towards hatchway, crashing into the half-shut opening with a massive boom, buckling it inwards. More trees are ripped from their roots, with plants and whirling boulders. I find my feet and sprint along the side of the dome, getting away from the scene of carnage, worried that I'll also be pulled through.

The hatchway is bombarded with rocks, branches, leaves and mud and is blocked again.

I've no idea how long it will last and quickly cross the ruined hemisphere towards the exit taking me into the park area.

The air is thin, but it's still breathable. I take small measured gasps, forcing my chest to move slowly—no matter how much it is screaming at me. I increase the blood flow to my lungs, ridding my corpuscles of carbon dioxide and infusing them with what little oxygen is left.

After ten long minutes of struggle, I make the further set of doors. Again, they stand open. I stagger through the small tunnel and into Elbaz's recreational dome. His cabin is still there, broken and partly collapsed, though it gives me hope of finding him alive. The lake and its fish are nothing more than a half-evaporated, half-frozen pool. I release the door mechanism, and hand-crank the doors shut. Silence. The sudden quiet is almost as disturbing as the escaping air. My body screams at me to rest, to sit down and go to sleep. I ignore the aches and pains and take in the scene of devastation. The park is unrecognizable—all the trees and well-tended plants are stripped bare of leaves, some of them shorn in two, others torn up by the roots. Just the cabin remains—a few beams and timbers.

I search around for Elbaz. It's possible he managed to anchor himself somewhere with a bottle of oxygen. But there's no sign of him. For the first time since the alarms went off, I'm inert… until I see a toe sticking out of the ice of the frozen lake.

Elbaz. It has to be.

I hurry over, knowing it's already too late.

He lies on his back, serene almost. Entombed. His snake-like eyes are open, as is his mouth. Drowned.

Elbaz was dead before the dome breach.

I'm not surprised. The person who tried to poison me murdered him to cover their tracks. The hydroponics expert knew who created the neurotoxin. Or at least would be able to guess at his or her identity.

I make my way quickly towards the conifer dome and the exit back to the base. Most of the trees are still standing, their evergreen stripped bare. I stumble through the forest and once again come across the glade. The black Ghost Orchids are gone. Delicate things. Easily destroyed by a sudden gust of wind. I search the clearing anyway.

Afterwards, I half-walk, half-stagger to the hatchway. I'm oxygen starved and starting to feel the deathly effects of the toxins in my system. And frankly, I'm dog-tired. A flashing red light tells me all I need to know. The door is locked. I take out my wafer and hit the broadcast button, knowing that I will hardly be able to speak in the thin atmosphere. I save my breath for a single sentence.

"This is Vatic, I'm by Elbaz's door. He's dead. Come and let me out."

rats

THE HATCHWAY opens. A rushing wall of air, red flashing lights and the sound of sirens, hits me as a slap in the face. The pressure difference between the two areas blows me backwards, but I struggle through, and find Offia waiting for me, her skin is pale, her eyes wired like mine… standing next to her is Bill.

"It took us a while to override the hatchway locking mechanism," he says, also pale and shaking. "Where's Elbaz?"

"He's gone," I gasp, taking in vast lungfuls of air. And, in seconds, my head begins to clear. Bill locks the hatchway into place and the noise of the depressurisation alarms stops, although the red lights continue to flash. I take out my wafer and hit 'Broadcast'. "This is Vatic. The breach was sabotage and Elbaz is dead. Everyone meet me in the Canteen now."

A crackle and Ackermann's reedy voice squeaks out of my handheld. *"What is all this nonsense?"*

"Do as I say. That's an order." I cut Ackermann off in the middle of a bark of expletives. I turn back to

Offia. "Let's go."

The counter is now flashing, the digits in the red: *0 hours, 36 mins.*

I'm weak, tired. My limbs heavy. The Boost is finally wearing off. I've not peed since I was in Frederix's shower and I've no desire to go now. Combined with the dull ache in my lower back, the answer is simple: kidney failure. My organs are shutting down as predicted.

Five minutes later, we arrive in the canteen. Director Frederix sits waiting, his arms crossed. Calculating eyes flick up at our entrance. I'm expecting a tirade, but he remains button-lipped.

Bill lowers me into one of the frail-looking chairs. "I'll make you something to eat."

"I've lost my appetite," I say. Maybe I've gone past hunger and exhaustion.

Bill ignores me. He powers up the galley. He's confused, stressed. I feel his emotions strongly. I guess he needs to be busy.

Food is the last of my concerns. I have to solve this damn puzzle and get off this barren rock.

Frederix says nothing. His eyes glare at the blank walls behind me. His demeanour speaks volumes, even if he is quiet. I'm in charge here, not the Director. 'Depressurisation protocols' or not. I'm fed up with playing games with him. If Frederix gets in my way again, I'll take him down. I may be less than half the man I used to be, but he's still no match for me. Thankfully, he seems too preoccupied to speak.

The sound of heavy breathing and similarly heavy footsteps and Ackermann enters the canteen. "What the hell is going on?" he yells at Frederix.

The Director maintains his quiet. I'm impressed. Up to now, Frederix has very much enjoyed his own voice.

"Address your questions to me," I say. "That fool has no authority here." I admit it. I'm goading Frederix. And why not? The Director's gaze doesn't change. I'm hoping he's a spent force. So far he's only tried to hinder my investigation—or that's what it feels like.

Ackermann's vast bulk turns towards me. "Elbaz?"

I shake my head.

He falls into a chair, nervously taking a box of cigarettes out of his pocket and lighting up. Smoking anywhere outside hydroponics in an oxygen-controlled environment is strictly forbidden. He doesn't seem to care and I realise the man is more than upset about the recent events—or he's a good actor. I nod to him and he slides the pack over. I flip out a cigarette and he lights it for me. "Depressurisation," he spits, the words hissing from his lips as a high whine. "What a terrible way to go." He sucks repeatedly on his cigarette as if it's a baby's teat.

I also take a drag. I keep the tobacco in my lungs for long seconds before I let the soothing vapours escape through my nose. "Don't be too disturbed," I say.

"What does that mean?" Ackermann shouts amidst a fog of expelled smoke. It floats around his head, hanging like a poisonous cumulonimbus cloud.

At that moment, Trinny Lunn appears. Her face is even whiter than usual. Up to now, I'd not realised the effect of the emergency on everyone. Hull breaches happen all the time. They're part of space living. You might say 'commonplace'. Fast moving bits of rock and debris too small to be seen on a scanner can hole the most protected haven. People train for depressurisation. They know what to do. They trust in the multi-layered hulls and auto-repair systems. The protocols make sense, of course they do. But this breach was like none other they had experienced or expected. For a start, the crisis went on for a helluva long time. And secondly, the much-vaunted safety systems all failed to work.

Lunn makes no pretence of talking to the Director. Frederix is finished and she knows it. I admire her intelligence as much as her practicality. She wafts Ackermann's smoke away with an annoyed hand but doesn't complain. These are exceptional circumstances. She looks at me, her eyes widening. "Your face?"

I rub my dead eye. The socket must be swollen again. "I had an argument with the security system, things got out of hand."

Trinny seems confused by my answer. She could be bluffing, but whatever ability I may have as an empath is now redundant, useless.

"Where's Elbaz?" she asks. She knows he's dead. After my broadcast on the wafer, they all do.

"He didn't make it."

Ackermann shifts his loose flesh in the confines of his chair. "I never liked the guy, but to die like that…"

"He drowned." My words hang on the air and I have to wait for a few seconds for everyone to digest them.

Offia sat upright. "Drowned?"

"It's very simple. Someone in this room killed him and then sabotaged his dome and the security protocols to cover their tracks."

My statement causes consternation. Ackermann looks like he might explode, whilst Trinny sits back in her chair, confusion dominating her delicate features, her head shaking in disbelief.

A clatter behind me makes everyone jump. Bill dropping a handful of cutlery on to the floor.

"Sorry," he says with embarrassment, putting another omelette in front of me and darting inquisitive eyes at Trinny Lunn. He sits down.

While they take in my news, I eat mechanically, smoking between mouthfuls. My hunger abandoned me a long time ago. A bad sign, but I need the energy—even if I only have minutes left.

Offia lights a shaky cigarette. "That's why you risked your life, isn't it?" she says, swallowing heavily. "That's why you went into Hassan's dome. To rescue Elbaz and learn what he knew."

I nod. "My gut told me the breach was sabotage and I wasn't proven wrong. I was hoping to find Elbaz alive and maybe some clues to what is going on here." I reach into my skinsuit and pull out one of Elbaz's mutated Ghost Orchids. It hasn't fared well. I place the ruined flower upon the table. Everyone stares at the half-decomposed, fleshy bloom—a black, man-shaped shrouded apparition perched atop a long, thin stalk. "You see my eye? I didn't get this from walking into a door, not exactly. Someone tried to kill me with a booby-trapped scanner. A needle filled with neurotoxin that came from Elbaz's lab—made from these flowers. Fortunately, for his murderer, Elbaz is now unable to tell us who that someone is."

I nod to Offia.

"Vatic gave me the toxin to test," the biologist says in her practical way. "All evidence pointed to the poison being plant-based," she continues. "A flower of the same genus as this one."

"You're saying you were attacked and Elbaz murdered?" Bill asks, his face a mix of incredulity and horror. "Why? What was their motive?"

I shrug. "My investigation was stumped. Yet somewhere along the way, I stepped on the killer's toes. They were worried I'd find out something about them. And, as you know, the Skilled always get their guy."

"I'm not sure I believe you, Mister Vatic," says Trinny Lunn. "No-one was murdered until you showed up. You are the only variable factor in this equation."

I round on her. "And what the hell does that mean?"

"You forget. I've seen your war record. If anyone is a killer on this base, it's you."

Her words cut into me. I don't care. I'm dying. "You didn't mind so much when you kissed me."

"You kissed him?" says Bill.

Trinny shrugs. "A little experiment."

Bill stands up, a peculiar expression on his face. "Vatic, can I have a private word?"

A flash of rage crosses Trinny's features. "Bill!

What on Earth are you doing? Sit down and be quiet!" she shouts.

Bill ignores her, as if she's not there.

"Are you listening to me?" Trinny shouts again. "We need to get him off this base! Bill!"

"If you know something," I say to Bill, "then I suggest you tell everyone."

The kid shakes his head and sits back down. Trinny stares at him angrily, a blush appearing on her high cheekbones.

I have no idea about the nature of their relationship, yet I get the impression Trinny thinks herself very much in control.

"Who do you suspect?" Bill asks quietly.

"Bill!" Trinny is almost shrieking.

Bill finally acknowledges the diminutive blond. "Let him speak… okay?"

Trinny draws breath, but says nothing.

I slide the last of the omelette into my mouth, swallow and take a final drag on the smoking stub of my cigarette. Offia snatches it from my fingers impatiently, stands up and throws it into the sink. She leans back on the kitchen-top and crosses her arms, her forehead furrowing. Large sparkling eyes flashing between Bill and Trinny Lunn.

"You want to know who I suspect?" I say.

Bill nods.

Frederix's head whips round. "Why don't I save you the trouble? Vatic thinks I'm the killer, don't you? He's had it in in for me since he arrived."

"You were certainly well-placed to interfere with the security system and the safety protocols and you didn't want me to enter Elbaz's labs during the emergency. That makes you a suspect." I shrug. "But from what I've learned about everyone here, you all have the capability."

The Director says nothing.

"Chen's death was nothing to do with me," Ackermann exclaims. "I didn't like Elbaz and I certainly dislike you, but why would I want to kill either of them?"

"To cover your tracks. Maybe you were frightened I'd report back to the company about your work… or shall I say, the lack of work."

Ackermann's eyes widen behind his glasses. "You little shit!"

I raise my fork threateningly. "Don't worry. You're not on your own. Elbaz's research was side-lined months ago. Offia has become nothing more than a company monkey—she's done no proper work for almost two years." I cast an apologetic glance in her direction, but she's distracted, like she's not listening. "The Director has been here since the project's beginning and has a reputation that should've had him replaced a long time ago. And we know Chen got the chop due to a lack of results. Which leaves Trinny and Bill."

Offia picks up the Ghost Orchid. If she is angry with me for revealing her secret, she doesn't show it. The muscles of her jaw bulge and I guess she is about to divulge what's on her mind.

"Before you go on, there's something I discovered," she says, her lip trembling. "Something we all need to know."

I lean back in my chair. The omelette sits heavily on my stomach. I feel like retching, but stifle the reflex.

"Vatic asked me to check Chen's blood for nanites," Offia says quietly. "A hunch of his and… I found them. Their presence is not important in itself—nanites are an accepted medical treatment for a range of conditions—although their use is limited. This knowledge niggled me. So, on a whim, I checked my own blood." She takes a deep breath. "I discovered exactly the same nanites. I've not undergone any recent medical procedure—any procedure I know about. I went straight back to the canteen and retrieved the napkin Ackermann used after Vatic stabbed him with the fork. And again, the same nanites. All three of us have had the identical medical procedure."

Ackermann whips the glasses off his face and massages the bridge of his nose, his eyes glancing between Trinny Lunn and Offia. "That's nonsense. I'd never allow those bloody little robots into my system," he says, his voice an accusatory whine. "She's lying—she has to be." He points a fat, stubby finger at Offia. "Where's your proof?"

Proof…

The word suffuses through my mind making all kinds of positive connections. And, like space dust blown away by a sudden solar flare, I see properly for the very first time. The killer is not important—he or she is not what my 'investigation' is about. That's an irrelevance, a red herring. Instead, I see the bigger picture. I now know what's been going on here. It all goes back to why the Company chose me to probe

Chen's death and why this investigation was arse-over-tit from the outset. I stand up onto shaky legs and address everyone.

"You want proof? It's here. I'm the proof. A damn living and breathing lie detector. I've been awake for a few hours now. I've found out I'm different, special—*Skilled*. I'm a mass-murdering war hero with the talent of getting the job done whatever the odds. More than that—above everything else—I'm a bloodhound brought in to sniff out truth from all the bullshit. And there is a helluva lot of bullshit going on here."

Ackermann draws breath to speak again. I cut him off. "It took me a while to piece everything together. I admit, I was side-tracked by my obsession that Chen's death was not as it seemed, the attempt on my life and the murder of Elbaz. I've been wondering why I was brought here—the Company doesn't employ their top man to solve a simple suicide—but that's not why they woke me from hypersleep. No. I'm here as part of an experiment. In fact... *you all are*. At some point, the Company deemed you were expendable. Like rats in a Company maze."

Frederix swivels around in his chair. "What the hell are you talking about?"

"Don't you understand yet? I bet that if Offia tested everyone here, she'd find the same nanites." I sit back down, reach for another of Ackermann's cigarettes, light up and take a drag. "Things have been amiss with me ever since I arrived at the Karst Base labs. At first, I thought this was due to disorientation. I wasn't connecting to people like I was used to. I put it down to the hypersleep, to my amnesia, to the fact I'm nearly starved to death. I should've listened more closely to my own insight. There's only one real person on this base. The rest of you are imposters."

Ackermann lurches to his feet, shouting. Bill, Trinny and Frederix remain seated. Offia stares away. She'd had more time to digest the information, to understand the implications.

"Let Vatic speak," Bill says quietly.

Ackermann sits back down, cursing.

I take a long thoughtful drag on my cigarette, watching the large man as he dutifully retakes his seat. "Everybody I talked to mentioned the Company's 'Holy Grails'. And one of those grails is the creation of artificial humanity… or at least something passing as human. Illegal of course, but if you can pull it off? Well, the sky's the limit. I wasn't brought in to investigate a possible suicide. No. I'm here to see how well everyone performs. To see if I would notice."

"Notice what?" says Offia, her face a mask of worry.

"…Notice who's real and who isn't."

Ackermann's fat hands ball into twin fists and I observe blood leaking from the wound I inflicted earlier. "You're talking absolute rubbish. I'm certainly not artificial, I mean, just look at me!"

Offia is as calm as I've ever seen her. Resigned almost. "It was the nanites. They altered us. You're dead, Ackermann. And so am I. We're all dead."

"Not everyone," I interject. "There is someone here who is not what they seem."

"And who the hell is that?" spits Frederix.

"I will come to him… or her in a minute."

"Don't tell me you're swallowing Offia's nonsense?"

Ackermann spat. "She's lying—she has to be. Lying to cover her own tracks is my guess."

"Unfortunately, Offia is telling the truth."

"There's no way you can know that."

"There's no way a normal human being can know… yet I'm not a normal human being am I?" I shake my head and continue. "So far, creating convincing androids is an unachievable goal. They are easily detected as artificial by the most basic of scanners and the simplest of humans. But what if the only synthetic part was …the brain itself?"

"Impossible!" blurts Ackermann. "Sure, we can miniaturise computers, but the problem is heat. A human system cannot be adapted to deal with those kind of temperatures. Even if the machine was built by nanites. And how would the thing be powered? Like I said: an impossibility."

"But what if you used bio-replacement nano-technology at the cellular level." I take another drag from my cigarette and blow smoke at Trinny Lunn. "Isn't that right, Trinny?" The thick, tobacco vapours curl around her blond hair. We both know she's been found out.

Frederix stabs me with his pale eyes. This time I glimpse hatred in them. A cold emotion, though dangerous all the same. "You believe Trinny has somehow replaced our brains and we have not noticed? You're a fucking idiot."

"That's exactly what she did. Or thinks she did."

The scowl leaves Trinny's face.

I give Trinny my full attention. "You don't know, do you?"

"What are you saying?"

"I'm saying, you're not who you think you are either."

"Don't be ridiculous. You're talking nonsense. The Company made a mistake in sending you. You're no empath, you're a mess." She stands up, pushing her chair over with anger. "I'm in charge of the Zeta-Karst Laboratories, no one else!"

I shake my head.

"Then who?"

"Why don't you ask Bill?"

All eyes turn to the kid. "He's the only true human here," I say. "And I'm counting myself in that sentence. I represent the mutant faction." Realisation dawns across everyone's faces, especially Trinny Lunn's. "In all the time I've been on Karst Base, Bill is the one I've felt closest too. For whom I've experienced the full human response—but that wasn't what I was looking for, was it? I was after a murderer. Bill didn't kill Elbaz, nor try to kill me. He's a murderer of a different type altogether."

Bill purses his lips and his features subtly alter. He's still the same fresh-faced kid, but his demeanour is no longer that of an underling. "Like I said Vatic, we need to talk."

"Bill?" Trinny says.

Bill shrugs.

"You bastard!" she shrieks, thumping at his chest and face with her small fists.

Bill doesn't move a muscle. "Sit down Trinny and shut up." His voice is measured, calm and sends a shiver down my spine.

Trinny acts like a puppet pulled by its strings and collapses into a chair.

"That's quite some trick," I say.

Bill shrugs. "I've a long career ahead of me. I saw an opening… and I'm ambitious."

Ackermann sags, his bloated face reddened and sweaty. Frederix says nothing. His eyes twitching between me and Bill.

"Oh fuck," says Offia. "Oh fucking fuck!"

I'm genuinely sorry for Offia. I like her, respond to her. But she's not human. Not anymore. None of them are. "So Bill, are you going to tell me how you did it?"

Bill reaches over for Ackermann's cigarettes and lights up. He appears changed. More mature. And I wonder if this is his true appearance. He could be any age masquerading as youth. A good disguise.

"Like I told you," he begins. "My work is in pure processing. Uncontaminated, unadulterated research. I'm one of the few geniuses the Company gives free reign to. My specialty is in human thinking systems with a side-line in miniaturisation. I went back to the basics. To brain cells. I studied their processes and connections. Their interaction in groups and ganglions; I examined how memory is laid down in arrays of proteins. And yes, I was able to replicate a human brain, but I couldn't make the artificial mind think. Nor could I shrink it to fit inside a regular skull. Nor, as you said, design it to be undetectable from the most basic of scanners. That was before I read Trinny Lunn's research on mechanical bio-replacement—substituting bone tissue with stronger, better materials by the use of cell-targeted nanites. Lunn never realised that her work could be utilised to replace brain synapses. Billions of them. Replicating neural pathways and memory RNA. Even duplicating the processes used by cells to power themselves. We met and, with full Company backing, we devised this little experiment."

"Some experiment."

"This base was a prime choice," Bill continues. "We already had Frederix and Elbaz. Two washed up losers soon to be given their marching orders.

"Watch it, Bill!" warns Frederix as Ackermann curses.

Bill ignores them. I guess, to him, they are lab rats. Expendable.

"The rest were easy to come by. Ackermann living off others' research, Offia, a top biologist caught using Company materials and equipment to make street drugs."

"And Chen?"

"Jelinek was the last to join us. An excellent test subject, before we moved on to the bigger fish." He flicked his eyes around the small group and smiled. "He was disturbed from the start—so who would notice if he became a little odder? The procedure was in its infancy then. Chen unfortunately suffered a complete mental breakdown—as we both discovered in his quarters."

Chen's repeated phrase 'I am Chen Jelinek' now makes sense. The man was a replacement and defective at that.

"We learnt a lot from Chen. And refined our

process. We realised there was no rush and slowed the procedure down. Feeding the nanites in a steady stream, replacing brain cells one at a time. So subtle that the subjects didn't even notice."

"I refuse to believe this!" spits Ackermann. "You're deranged, you're—"

"Bark like a dog," Bill says simply.

Ackermann draws an indignant breath and tries to speak. The result is a series of high-pitched yaps.

Bill raises his hand. "Silence."

Ackermann's mouth keeps moving, his voice nothing more than the mechanical sounds of his flexing jaw. He flushes, turning purple with rage. Tears appear in the corners of his eyes from which the light seems to suddenly drain.

Bill smiles, pleased with this display. "The control of test suspects was a little harder to master. Elbaz, for instance, was fiercely independent. But we realised even someone like him could be broken. Offia was a walkover, as was the Director."

Frederix doesn't move a muscle. He just stares at Bill. Unblinking.

"And Trinny Lunn?"

"She was always going to be a part of the experiment. A last test before the final examination. She had no idea until just now. I'd say… that was a success."

Trinny sits shaking at the table, her eyes wired and full of horror.

I take a deep breath and fix Bill with my remaining eye. "And I'm part of the final examination also. You needed to see if your replacements could pass muster in front of one of the Skilled. So you got the Company to send their best man. Me."

"The Company were keen to find out how effective the technique was. First off they wanted to know if it was possible to order one of my subjects to commit suicide."

"Chen."

"Yes, and he obliged. And as soon as he killed himself, the Company sent that idiot, Strategist Stranng to go wake you up. Things will not go well for him when I report back. Once I found out what he did—kicking you out into space without oxygen—his days are numbered. I'm personally going to make sure he is demoted and expelled."

"And my role was to see if I could spot your little charade."

"That's right. I was worried you were not up to the task. That you were too far gone. You surprised me."

"How did you administer the nanites?"

Bill gestures to the galley area. "It's not my fault I'm a good cook. The nanites can be hidden in anything. Water sacs, tea, coffee or… an omelette."

I look down at my plate and shake my head. "Not me. You needed my mind intact."

"No, not you Vatic. I offered you the chance to talk, yet you refused. Your work here is now done. Offia, Ackermann grab him!"

Ackermann lurches from his chair and knocks me to the floor, trapping me with his vast weight, while Offia, holds my arms, her eyes flashing at me with a look of dismay.

"Your experiment failed, Bill," I gasp. "I recognised

your replacements. You're done. Washed up. Any other Skilled from any other company will also see through this sham."

"You think my research is over? I don't give up that easily. A few more tweaks and I'll try again. You're not the only Skilled the Company has access to."

"What about Elbaz? What about the attempt on my life? Have you forgotten there's a killer amongst your rats?"

A frown crosses Bill's face.

"Isn't it obvious?" I say. "You have replicated a murderer. Down to the last psychopathic brain cell."

Behind Bill, Frederix slowly raises himself to his feet. There's something in the way his face is moving—his stance and the hand in his pocket—that sends a siren blaring through my cerebral cortex. He produces a gun. An old-fashioned six-chamber revolver. Before I can say anything, he pistol-whips Bill who crumples to the floor in a dead faint. The Director then stabs the muzzle at the back of Ackermann's head and pulls the trigger. The roboticist's enormous face explodes outwards, showering me in blood and brains. Frederix turns to Offia, shooting her twice in the chest before pointing the gun at me...

...In that moment, I slow everything down. It takes a massive surge of energy, but while talking, I was also concentrating on absorbing as much from my recent meal as possible. I see the explosion as the firing pin hits the bullet, the projectile emerging from the barrel, flying towards me. Even with my reflexes and mental processes speeding as fast as they are, muscle is slower to react. I try anyway, whipping my head to one side, but I will not be able to dodge the—

BLACKNESS

irenka

I AWAKE in the dark, frozen to the marrow—shivering like having a fit, my head pounding and my heart thumping fast in my ears. I'm lying on a cold, hard floor. Something is wrong with the gravity—or the lack of it. A single sharp memory stabs into my mind… *I've been shot!*

I bring my hand up to my temple, wincing at my icy fingers, and find a large bump. The bullet must have given me a glancing blow only. The movement of my arm is enough to send me skirting off sideways along the floor. Wherever I am, the artificial grav is turned off. I hit something soft. Another body propped up against a wall. Large, bulbous and covered in congealed blood. A name floats into my consciousness: Ackermann. And my memory, or what's left of it, returns…

Bill, the kid who I trusted, revealed as some kind of mastermind, his head bashed in shortly afterwards… Frederix the murderer all along.

With what I now know about Bill and Trinny's experiment, I realise I had no chance of detecting

Frederix. He's a psychopath. I can usually spot such social misfits by their emotional detachment, or their inability to fully disguise themselves. That was my problem from the start. After Trinny's nanites, everyone appeared emotionally distant. Offia and the rest were near-perfect copies, and with nothing to compare them to, other than Bill who I purposely ignored, I was always going to struggle.

Frederix obviously thinks I'm dead. I suppose I looked the part—unconscious and covered in Ackermann's brains. I run my frozen fingers over the bump on my head again. The swelling is the size of a duck's egg, but just a bruise. I've survived worse. A quick check of the blood vessels and the pressure in my skull tells me I've nothing to worry about. I slow my heartbeat all the same. I have far more immediate concerns—I need to find out where I am and get the hell out of here.

I sit up, being very careful in the low gravity and suddenly I'm reeling. Dizzy, disorientated and my vision full of stars. "Not good, Vatic," I croak to myself. "Not good at all." I remember the wafer. I had the handheld in my skinsuit when I entered the canteen, pressed close to my skin. I take it out and swipe the screen into life…

0 hours, 0 mins.

The readout is no longer flashing. What did the Medic back on the ship say?

"Six hours before your organs start giving up. You may last a further hour, if you're lucky."

I'm still alive and living on borrowed time. The wafer tells me there's no mainframe, no systems to connect to. The whole base must be off-line.

The illuminated rectangle puts out enough light for me to see another figure in the gloom, also perched against the wall: Trinny Lunn. She's dead. Shot in the head and neck, her perfect features now ugly and distorted. Frederix has not just dumped her here. Both Lunn and Ackermann are posed—sitting on opposite sides of a small square room, seemingly looking towards the centre where I was lying. As for Bill—with what he knows—my bet is Frederix is gonna sell him off to one of the rival companies. He'd be set up for life.

I look for Offia. She's not here with us. I don't hold out much hope for her, she took two bullets in the chest at close range. Her death saddens me the most. Copy or not, I liked her. I realise now… she reminds me of the girl I killed, Esta. The Skilled who was fool enough to love me.

I shake my head, now is not the time to be thinking about her, about what I've done. My terrible past.

The weak beam of my makeshift torch reveals a pair of skulls glued back to back, a folded skeleton encased in a neat plastic bag; mummified feet, cut off at the ankles and bound in handcuffs and numerous other atrocities. I've heard of places like this: 'Ritual Rooms'.

One wall is full of stuffed creatures of various types mimicking human poses. Trade in animals dead or alive is illegal unless you have the money or the influence—but then again if Elbaz was able to procure flora and faunae for his hydroponic domes, it wouldn't be too much of a stretch for someone to take advantage of him or his supplies. And I now know who that someone is: Director Anton Frederix. I notice a well-used bed in the corner—Frederix actually slept in here—the reason why his rooms were so unlived in and antiseptic.

Another figure, smaller in stature, petite—almost childlike—hangs on the wall in an attitude of crucifixion. A woman naked except for a loincloth. Her cheeks are sunken in death, her eyes replaced by glass, the skin laminated and shiny. She wears a crown of thorns with theatrical blood painted upon her brow. A knife protrudes from her side, the same, bright red crimson paint staining the blade. A name flits through my mind: *Irenka*. The undergarment I found in Frederix's quarters belonged to her—or so he'd said. And now I understand.

She never left the base.

By the looks of things, Frederix is a serial killer. Calculating and meticulous. I guess he's only been playing at the part of the anally-retentive Director. He's managed to keep his dark secret for quite some time. Until I turned up. It was my interest in Irenka that caused him to act. My investigation highlighted Irenka's disappearance—her murder. That's why Frederix tried to kill me by booby-trapping the eye-scanner and why he killed Elbaz and sabotaged his labs. I can only speculate, but Irenka's killing must've been unplanned. He'd messed up with the intern and knew he was on borrowed time. Sooner or later, someone would notice she was missing. That's why he had the gun with him in the canteen. He was going to kill us all regardless of Bill's admission.

Irenka hangs on the wall by what appears to be a door. I stumble over and look for an opening mechanism before realising the knife in Irenka's side is actually some kind of grim handle. I grab the hilt, feeling the blade flex downward. A click and the door opens, and as it does so, Irenka speaks. The sound is nothing more than a croak, a strangled whisper...

Anton.

But it's enough to send me reeling backwards. I twist and fall over in the low gravity, flying across the room, crashing into Trinny. It takes a few seconds for me to realise what happened, to comprehend the full horror—Irenka is still alive. Although, judging by her present condition, it's probably only a half-life. Something to keep Frederix amused. Either way, Irenka is gone, finished.

I lay Trinny down, crossing her hands respectfully over her chest and go back to the crucified woman, putting my ear against her lips. She whispers four words. "I love you, Anton."

I have no idea how Frederix is keeping her alive or if she is alive at all. But I do know she doesn't really love him. This is another part of his own personal horror show. He most likely drugged and kidnapped her, before…

I reply in the only way I can. "I'll try my best to release you."

She attempts to speak, but I can't make out the word. She repeats it, and this time it escapes from her unmoving mouth as a breathless sigh: "…Frederix."

"You won't suffer for much longer," I say before pulling open the door.

I'm met by a staircase leading upwards. At the top, a trapdoor. I find a handle and push. Something large slides aside and I crawl out, sweeping my makeshift torch. I'm back in Frederix's lab, emerging from under one of his experiment tanks—the one I'd spotted before the breach. Did he know I was close to discovering his secret? Either way, I forced him to act.

I go over to the hatchway. The door is open. Frederix must have cut the power to the whole base—in such a situation, all doors are automatically unlocked. I have one ace up my sleeve—Frederix doesn't know I'm alive. I'm Vatic. The Skilled who refused to be killed. He should've made sure of my death with a second bullet. The man is cocky, overconfident and a copy.

I lean on the door to catch my breath and try to put myself in Frederix's position. *What is his plan?* There's no way he can stay on the base. Not now. And, with what's inside his head, the Company would never let him escape. They'd hunt him across the galaxy to stop his brain falling into the wrong hands.

But I'm getting ahead of myself. Up to a short while ago, the Director—or I suppose the 'ex-Director' as I can now call him—had no idea what was going on here at this base. He'd killed Irenka and was about to be unmasked as a murderer. So why the breach? Why not just kill everyone and disappear...?

Unless...? No, he wouldn't, *would he?*

I have to admit that, although horrified, I'm impressed. The man is a class-one lunatic, but it's something I'd have thought of myself. He's gonna blow the base. Plain and simple. He's shut everything down. Well nearly everything. Every Company installation has a self-destruct. A way to destroy incriminating evidence or to make sure vital research does not fall into the hands of rival persons or organisations. The breach alerted the Company there was a problem, and when they hear nothing back, they'll come to investigate and find nothing but a debris field.

And Frederix? He's probably arranged a ship to pick him up.

The plan is simple, logical and cold. Perhaps we're not so different, him and me, after all. I underestimated him from the outset. He played the petty Director with aplomb. There's a lot more to Frederix than I realised—why else incapacitate Bill so quickly after he understood what was going on here? He'd seen how the others had been ordered around like puppets and wasn't about to let that happen to him.

But it's my survival that concerns me now. If Frederix is still on the base, where would he be? Again, I put myself into his shoes. He'd be suited up, ready to leave. "You're by the airlock."

Within minutes, I'm stumbling into the canteen and grabbing a carving knife. Then I'm bounding easily in the low gravity through the cold, black corridors. On the way, I shut down the neural pathways that deliver all the nasty, unwanted information from my body. I know I'm dying, but there's no reason why I should suffer. I carry on regardless, my limbs struggling to move. Mercifully, in this gravity, I'm almost floating as it is. I come to a slow halt and gingerly peer into the Auxiliary Hub.

And there he is. Frederix. I see him crouching inside the airlock compartment, right next to the outer door. Another figure lies unmoving behind him, attached by a line.

It's Bill, it must be.

Frederix wears a full spacesuit and helmet, complete with manoeuvrability pack. For a second, I wonder what he's doing before I see he's about to blow the airlock. With Karst Base in shutdown, there's no way for him to escape unless he uses the explosive charges inbuilt for such situations. It's not unexpected, but I'm without oxygen and a mask.

Nothing happens. I check Frederix more closely. His hand is on the release, but he's waiting for his rescue ship. I quietly grab a cylinder of air and strap the bottle to my side. There's no more manoeuvrability packs that I can see, but that doesn't matter now. I put on the helmet and start the oxygen.

I realise my mistake at once. I hear Frederix breathing over the suit radio—the helmets are on an open circuit.

Frederix flicks his head around and stares right at me. If he's surprised, the emotion doesn't register on his helmet-lit face. He takes in my knife and smiles. "You sure are hard to get rid of, but there's no way you're going to survive what's coming next."

Even over the comlink, I can hear the difference in his voice. Gone is the petty, effeminate and erudite Director with the lazy drawl. In his place is someone infinitely more sinister.

"At least I'm not a copy. That must be a drag."

"I don't care either way. That jumped up kid won't be ordering me around."

I advance on him.

"Don't even think about it, Vatic."

"If you blow the door, both of us are gonna be sucked out into space."

He tilts his head downwards and I see he's secured himself. I take in the information with a mouthed 'damn it'. "I saw Irenka… nice."

"She was a lot of fun."

"At least she will be out of her misery soon."

"Shame you pushed on that one. Made me show my hand."

"Sounds like you were a little messy if all it took was the threat of a check to find out she'd gone missing."

"You said so yourself: *the Skilled always get their guy.* But I planned this escape long before you turned up. I was tired of playing the Director and besides, I fancied a change. You just sped things along a little, and the idea of offing the Company's top investigator appealed to me."

"The eye-scanner was primitive. So was drowning Elbaz."

Frederix shrugs. "Elbaz had been growing his mutated ghost orchids for over a year. He knew his head was on the chopping block and those plants were his exit plan."

"I'm not sure what you mean."

"He was processing the blooms and stockpiling the neurotoxin. My guess is he planned to release his poison into the atmosphere as soon as they came to close him down."

"How did you find him out?"

"He liked to drink whisky. And as you noticed yourself, I have a decent supply. That mixed in with some drug inducements of my own concoction and he told me everything. I guessed something was up—I'd known him for years—he was wound so tight. The next day he woke up with a sore head and no idea what he'd said. It wouldn't have been hard for Elbaz to put two and two together once he learnt it was his neurotoxin that blinded you."

"And that's why you killed him."

"As soon as you survived my little booby-trap, I knew I was on limited time. Blowing up Elbaz's lab was always part of my exit plan. Makes the system wide failure look more plausible, don't you think? Drowning the idiot was just icing on the cake."

"And Bill and Trinny, their experiment?"

For the first time in this exchange, a look of embarrassment mixed with anger crosses Frederix's face. "I thought they were, you know, *at it*. I admit—I didn't realise the full scale of their plans together. That we were all rats in their little experiment. It took you to work that out. For which I'm thankful."

"What's it like?" I ask. "Being dead."

Frederix's breath rasps over the radio. "I feel no different. I'm the same me. I'll have plenty of time to process the news and besides, I've got Bill. He'll fetch a pretty penny. And you never know he might be able to reverse the procedure… or enhance it."

All the time we have been talking, I've been steadying myself. Throwing a knife in low gee is a very different experience than normal gravity. I'll only have one chance. "I suppose you're gonna sell to the highest bidder?"

"Yep. As soon as I'm on board my ship, I'll be making a few calls."

"Do you think the Company will let you get away with this? They'll hunt you down until they get back what is rightfully theirs."

"They'll be none the wiser. My transport is arriving at any moment. And when it does—this place is gonna go boom-boom. No evidence anybody survived. And that includes the Company's top investigator." He holds up a flashing wafer.

I grip the hilt of the knife readying myself, but the movement is not missed.

"You think you can throw your blade before I blow the airlock?" Frederix asks.

"He won't have to!" A familiar voice on the helmet radio.

There's a sound like an explosion played backwards and Frederix's upper torso disintegrates.

detonations

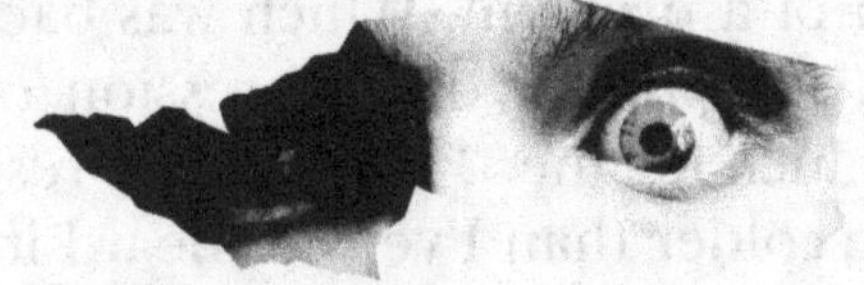

"I SHOULDN'T be surprised you survived a shot to the head—you seem the stubborn type," Offia says, her voice crackly over the radio. "You sure don't kill easily."

I twist around to see her standing in the hatchway holding a smoking flashgun in one hand, the other planted on the curve of her hip. She's wearing a tight-fitting green-tinted skinsuit, capped with a green helmet. A custom job, complete with matching manoeuvrability pack.

"What the hell!" I blurt, unable to control my words.

"I don't kill that easily either. Which is lucky for at least one of us." She glides over to what's left of Frederix and retrieves his flashing wafer, kicking him aside with a nonchalant foot. The lower half of the ex-Director's body bounces away into the dimness. She unclips Bill's cable and attaches the wire to her own belt.

"We need to contact the Company," I say. "And tell them their little experiment didn't work."

Offia lifts her firearm and points the still red-hot muzzle at me. Flashguns are highly dangerous and very illegal. Such weapons can smash a human apart at the molecular level. With Offia's connection to the black market, I guess getting her hands on one was not much of a problem. Which was bad luck for Frederix and, judging by the expression on Offia's face, no good luck for me. "This aint no rescue," she says, her voice colder than I've ever heard it.

"What do you mean?"

"My real name isn't Offia Okonjo."

"Seems there's a lot I don't know about you. Particularly how you managed to survive two shots to the chest."

"It certainly smarted. But in the same way you always wear a skinsuit, I always wear my flak vest. Not very flattering, granted, but I grew up with it. We still had old-fashioned guns and knives back in the Projects. I never went anywhere without protection. It saved my life on quite a few occasions. A lucky habit. I'm just as lucky Frederix didn't shoot me in the head."

"The Projects?"

Her green helmet nods.

"You escaped from the Red Planet?"

Offia smiles, her voice calm. "Yeah. One of the few."

The Mars' Projects were a black mark over Earth history. Thousands of colonists were flown out to the fourth planet, promised land and the resources to make a pioneering life. But the economic climate changed and they were left stranded in the makeshift accommodation provided for them at disembarkation. And the situation only got worse. Every week more transports arrived bringing even more colonists Earth wouldn't let return. The result was famine, disease, and outright anarchy. The shanty town of Syrtis Major somehow survived over the next two hundred years to become a den of corruption and low-life. 'The Mars' Projects' as it was known by Earth, was put out-of-bounds. The people deemed too volatile, too dangerous. Somehow they survived, and it seemed... occasionally escaped. "And you hid that from the Company? I'm impressed."

"They never found me out, although they must've known about the drugs—that's why I was put in Bill's little experiment. I should've been happy, content in my new life as a Company Biologist. I went too far. I've always tinkered with stims—my trade, back on Mars. But even I was unprepared for the success of Boost. My undoing. But you know what they say... *you can take the girl out of the Projects, but you can't take the Projects out of the girl.*" She laughed, a sudden explosion of sound. "Still, you don't grow up in that pit of scum without learning how to survive. But I'm more than a survivor, a lot more."

"So how'd you escape Frederix?" I ask, my eyes tracking between the flashgun and Offia's helmeted face.

As soon as he disappeared to go shut down the base, I got the hell out of there. It's not the first time I've had to play dead. I'm sure the Director assumed I was wounded, that I'd crawled off somewhere to die on my own. He under-estimated me like a lot of other people."

"And so here we are. Frederix is half the man he used to be and Bill is under wraps. And you're pointing a gun at me. I've gotta ask... what's your next move?"

"You've put me in a tricky situation, that's for sure. You know I liked you."

"You're using the past tense."

"Hey, I offered you some candy, but you didn't want to eat. That kind of thing hurts a girl. Let's say you had your chance and blew it."

"Do I get a second chance?"

Another shake of her head.

"It's like that, huh?"

"I'm afraid so. But talking of second chances... Frederix had the right idea. I was listening to you two chatting over the radio. I hated the Director, yet his plan will still work. With one minor change." She pulls on the cable attached to Bill, who I see is now awake and struggling. His arms are bound to his sides, his legs tied together. He tries to shout, the sound a muffled scream.

"Looks as if Frederix gagged the kid. No way he's making me bark like a dog. Still, he has one use—he's going to make me very, very rich. Which means..."

"No loose ends?"

"I'm sorry, Vatic. Nothing personal, but unless you're coming with me, I can't let you get out of here alive. You know that."

"Then why bother saving me?"

"Like I said, this isn't a rescue. Thanks for distracting the Director for me by the way. Now, are you with me or not?"

"I thought I'd blown my chances?"

"A girl can change her mind, can't she? What do you say?"

"You really think Bill's work should continue? That he should be allowed to repeat what he did to you to thousands of others?"

Offia shrugged. "I'll be paid millions for his research… but you're not answering my question. Come with me. Partner up. I kinda like you and I think you like me."

She's offering me redemption. A way to change my life. She's a fake, and dangerous, but I also like her. She reminds me of Esta—the one good thing that has ever happened to me in this excuse for an existence. The girl I murdered all those years ago. Why shouldn't I go?

"You better hurry up. Frederix's ship can arrive at any time. And I'll have to blow the hatch." She clips herself to the wall.

My whole being is screaming at me to say 'yes'. To give in. To leave this life behind. So what if Bill's research kills thousands? *I've killed millions*. If I can live with those people on my conscience, what's a few more?

A crackle of static. "Zeta-Karst, come in."

Offia turns towards me. "Well?"

I shake my head.

A single heartbeat and Offia answers. "We're on our way."

I drop down, trying to find something to grab onto. Too late. Offia blows the lock and I'm sucked out of the hatchway, spinning like a top. The force of the explosion throws me tumbling and bouncing along the asteroid's surface, and I'm reminded of my first encounter with the base. This time there's no Bill to catch me. I'm on my own. I throw out my arms, flattening myself, increasing the drag of my body, digging my fingers into the thick dust. And, slowly, I manage to check my forward momentum and bounce to a measured stop. I twist around just in time to see Offia exit the airlock dragging Bill behind her. A quick puff of vapour from her manoeuvrability pack and she launches into space.

"You still alive?" Offia says over the radio.

I say nothing, although she must be able to hear my breathing.

"I'm gonna blow the base as soon as we're at a safe distance. So this is goodbye. You're a stubborn fool, Vatic. I'm sorry."

There's nothing else I can do—I have to sacrifice my oxygen. I take a deep breath and disconnect the bottle. I point the open nozzle toward the asteroid's surface and release the precious gas as a stream of vapour. I'm propelled upwards like a rocket and hurtled into the cold void of blackest space.

The sun of this solar system is far away. More like a bright star than the centre of this particular part of space. And, other than the torch-like comet, only a few distant suns pepper the cosmos. Faster-than-light travel is one of the crowning achievements of the human race, an amazing feat, but in reality, no-one really knows where they are anymore. Sure, we recognise Earth and its associated planets. Some of us actually get to visit our ancestral home, but all the other systems? They could be anywhere. I have no idea of the location of the Karst asteroid, or the distance of this solar system from Earth. Hyperspace is beautiful blur of flashing stars, a passage through a kind of non-space and then you've arrived. And like most modern wonders, we forget to marvel at the technology involved. At the hundreds of years of endeavour leading to our present technological dominance. That's very human, very normal...

As is dying.

A flash of light and a ship, like a giant, albino spider drops out of its cloak. I don't recognise the design—the cruiser must be an independent or a bootlegger. Knowing Frederix, it's probably a pirate. Offia will need to be careful. The ship moves purposely towards the rapidly diminishing dot that is Offia and Bill.

I look below me, I'm possibly ten miles away from Karst. I release more precious oxygen to increase my speed. But there's no way I'm going to get to a safe distance. And if I do... what then? I twist back and stare at the outlandish craft—long, white legs radiate from a gently glowing central mass. I can no longer make out Offia. She and Bill are lost in the blackness. To my right I see the comet shimmer. Its brilliance still dominates this region of space—a shining torch of white. But why is it shimmering?

My mind makes the obvious connection in the same moment as a Company ship drops out of hyperspace directly in front of me. Seconds later, the voice of Strategist Strang thunders over my radio.

"Vatic! What the hell is going on?"

"No time," I gasp. "The other ship, you've got to destroy it. Now!"

"On who's authority?"

"On mine, on the Company's! Do it, you've got seconds."

"I can't just fire on a defenceless spacecraft!"

"You don't like me, Stranng. I know that. You hate the Skilled. Yet you must be aware of what I've done. Of who I am. Destroy the ship now."

"You'd better not be wrong about this."

The Company vessel twists in front of me, the weapons array swinging into action. A series of flashes, an explosion and Offia's rescue ship is no more.

"Offia! I shout. "Are you out there?"

A crackle on the radio.

"Offia!" A click and I hear breathing. "You're alive. We'll come and get you."

"No."

The word is simple and quietly spoken, but it speaks with the certainty of the grave.

"You've no options left. I can still make this good for you."

"We could have had it all, Vatic. You and me. Yet you threw it away. There's no way I'm going back to the Projects. I promised myself that it if it came to it, I'd make sure I'd never return. And besides, I'm already dead."

Stranng bursts in over our conversation. "Let the bitch kill herself if she wants."

"You don't understand. She's gonna blow the base."

"What?"

"Offia, you don't have to do this."

"Oh… Vatic."

"Stranng!" I blurt. "Jump out of here, now!"

"We're going nowhere until—"

A flash behind me puts the yellow, modular boxlike ship into sharp relief. I turn to see a rapidly expanding, luminescent ball. Karst is no more, destroyed by a nuclear detonation that will consume us in moments. And then I'm hit, but not by the blast. It takes me a moment to realise I've been scooped up by a grappling arm.

"Hold on Vatic, this is going to be rough!"

I'm spun around and slammed into the body of the ship, allowing me to see the upcoming shockwave. It's almost upon us when… the universe is turned upside down and inside out.

earth

THE FIRST thing I'm aware of is a lack of pain. I'm numb and… comfortable. Lying in a bed of some kind.

"Vatic? You awake?"

I immediately recognise the voice. The female Medic. "I'm not sure," I croak. "You tell me."

"What the hell happened to you down there?"

Behind her voice, the hum of a Company spaceship. I'm inside and alive. "The investigation wasn't as straightforward as I anticipated."

"I gathered that."

"How am I doing, Doc? Last time I checked, I was half-blind and nearly dead."

"You'll be pleased to know that I've done a full blood scrub. Your organs should be working fine again. As for your right eye… it was shot to pieces. I had to take it out. You can get a replacement anytime, so I wouldn't worry too much. How'd you lose it?"

"I was attacked by a flower. Nasty." I open my good eye. The Medic stands over me, her thick red hair is washed and bushy, the grey replaced with strawberry-blond highlights. Her skin is shiny, whilst her green eyes are gently shaded with make-up. "You did all that for me? I'm honoured."

A smile on her thin lips reveals dazzling white teeth. "Maybe. Or maybe we've been summoned to Company headquarters back on Earth."

A creak of metal upon metal and in strides Stranng. "The Company are going bloody spare about Karst. What happened down there? And if I find out you've used me in any way, I'll throw you out of the airlock again, this time without a mask."

I push myself up on to my elbows. Stranng stands by the door, two CPs on each shoulder. "Relax. Whether I like it or not, I've turned you into a goddam hero. You may be a prick, but the Company are gonna be well-pleased when we reach Company HQ. We lost the base, but you stopped valuable information from getting into rival hands."

"Watch your mouth, Vatic, or—"

"Or what?"

"I've learned never to trust a Skilled—and I don't trust you now."

"So why did you fire on the ship?"

Stranng says nothing, and suddenly, unlike back on Karst with those manufactured replicates, I can read him. "You had to follow my orders, didn't you?"

Stranng remains silent, although his face speaks volumes.

"What is my rank?" I ask quietly.

"You don't have a commission. You're Vatic. A Skilled. And we all know they're done and finished within the Company."

"Don't lie to me, Stranng."

"What?"

"Give me your handheld."

He glares at me for a second before handing over the wafer.

The Medic appears confused and also impressed.

I swipe my fingers over the screen and bring up my full record. I see the face again. Maybe I'll get both eyes replaced. I've had enough of my cold, blue, wired stare. I flick through a few more pages and hand the wafer back to Stranng. "Take a look."

Stranng grabs the handheld, though his gaze stays fixed on me.

"Read it!"

Stranng drops his head to stare at the screen, his jaw clenching, the muscles in his cheeks bulging.

"What does it say?" My voice is almost a whisper.

Stranng's piggy eyes are full of resentment. "Vatic. Rank—Second… *Second Executive.*"

I nod my head. "I was in charge from the start, as soon as I came on board. Luckily for you and the Company, I didn't remember—or more importantly—I didn't realise that my commission was still active. I'd been away for too long. I'd almost forgotten. But, there…" I jab my finger at the wafer. "I'm a bona-fide member of the Secondary Executive. Outranking you and nearly everyone in the Company. And you threw me into space without any oxygen. CPs," I say with authority. "Strategist Stranng is under arrest. Place him in the airlock. I'll come deal with him later."

The two CPs grab him by the arms and drag him away.

"The airlock? You can't do this!" he shouts.

"I think you know I can… and you might want to suit up. I'll make a decision about giving you oxygen later on."

Stranng is dragged out of the room and door shuts with a clang.

"You're not really going to throw Stranng into space… are you?" says the Medic as his cries diminish into the distance.

"It's the same as what he did to me, remember? And I did promise myself to get even with that jumped up bastard—if I ever got the chance. But don't worry. I just want to make the man stew for a while. He deserves it. And besides, I wasn't lying. Stranng will be promoted off this ship very soon. Which is probably a relief for you and everyone else. He did good out there. Saved all our lives. When it came down to it, he followed orders like any decent Company man."

The Medic smiled.

"We're really going to Earth?"

"Yeah," she says. "It's my… my first time."

I search my memories. I've visited on many occasions. "The Third Planet is like nowhere else, although everyone is damn arrogant. But if you want to work there, I can try and arrange something."

"Anywhere off this bloody ship would be a relief." She shines a light into my good eye. "You're quite different without the hair and beard."

She leans in, her breath close and I realise I've never asked her name. "What do they call you?"

"Shipboard Medic Number One."

"You know what I mean."

"I'm Shereena… and you, what's your first name?"
"Me? I'm Vatic… *just Vatic.*"

Do you want a sneak preview of
Book Two, *Shattered Web*?
Then read on for the first few chapters of
Vatic's next mystery...

Or buy it now:

http://books2read.com/shatteredweb

*(full online store links for your country of residence
including Amazon, Apple, B&N,
Google, KOBO and more)*

Reviews

If you enjoyed reading *Shattered Web*, can I ask you to please leave a review. This is not just for me and other readers, but for a whole host of other boring marketing reasons that I won't go into right now.

Suffice it to say, if you leave me a review on any of the e-book stores, or Goodreads or anywhere else, I'll be *well-chuffed*, and it will certainly increase the likelihood of further novels in this and other series.

Thanks in advance!

For information on further releases, please join my newsletter *http://mostlywriting.com/join*

Or you can pop over to my Mostly Readers Facebook Group (*https://www.facebook.com/groups/mostlyreaders*). It's a friendly fun place to hang out.

Please read on for full details.

About *Shattered Helix*

First of all, I'd like to thank you for picking up *Shattered Helix*. I love this story for a lot of reasons, but mainly because this was my first *full-on* mystery novel—a breakthrough of sorts that has ultimately put me on the path towards more mystery writing. Most of my stories are mysteries anyway, but *Shattered Helix* took that genre and ran with it.

I never expected this novel to be anything more than a short story as part of my compilation *The Lady In The Glass: 12 Tales of Death & Dying*. I thought *a space mystery murder thing*, as I originally titled it, would be just right for this collection of novellas and shorts. I had a target of 8,000 words and no more. But Vatic had other ideas. Not only does he railroad everybody in the story, he also railroaded me. And I'm glad he did.

The name, *Vatic*, seemingly came from nowhere. I conjured it up with the full intention of changing it at a later date, but it stuck. I was very surprised to find out it is a Latin word for *prophet* or *oracle*. I sometimes wonder if these things are serendipitous, or the by-product of an active subconscious—either way, I'm always grateful.

So, secondly, I must give some credit to Vatic himself. I'm not sure where he came from, but he arrived fully formed on the page without any forethought or planning from myself.

Part of my technique is to put pen to paper (or fingertips to plastic) and see where I go. This novel was the result of such a process. I had this germ of an idea—of someone forcibly woken out of hypersleep—and Vatic emerged screaming into the world. It sounds odd to say that Vatic 'told the story to me' but that's what happened. On some days it was hard to keep up with him, particularly on some of the more 'adventurey' bits.

However, the story wasn't also without its angst. I remember getting close to the end of the mystery and, like Vatic himself, feeling no closer to the solution than at the beginning.

A terrible, empty, sick feeling.

And then—in a blast of light from the writery gods—the solution came to me. A perfect way to link everything up. *To solve the damn mystery!*

Those days when you have that one, single, startling breakthrough, make up for those less exciting days of hard slog, boredom and self-doubt. I live for them.

I've been amazed by the reaction to this novel and by the many emails, tweets and posts I've received since its publication. In many ways, it's a dream come true, to write, publish and get such wonderful feedback

Many of you have been asking about a sequel and...
it's here! The first four chapters of *Shattered Web: Vatic Book Two* can be found below.
Many thanks for reading *Shattered Helix*

All the very best,

Kev

Acknowledgements

Many thanks for the editing skills of:

Suzanne Buist
Caroline Bean
Dee J. Holmes
Blossom Young

Also by *K.J.Heritage*

Mystery and Crime
>Dying Is Easy
>The Peculiar Case of the Missing Mondrian

Science Fiction
>Shattered Helix *(Vatic Book 1)*
>Shattered Web *(Vatic Book 2)*
>Blue Into The Rip
>Quick-Kill & The Galactic Secret Service
>The Lady In The Glass - 12 Tales Of Death & Dying

Sci-Fi Compilations
>Once Upon A Time In Gravity City
>Chronicle Worlds: Legacy Fleet
>From The Indie Side

Fantasy
>The Scowl

Non-Fiction
>All About Copywriting: 55 Easy Edits To Improve Your Writing Forever
>3000 Writing & Plot Prompts A-C: Supercharge Your Creativity & Improve Your Writing Forever!

Find all ebooks, paperbacks, hardbacks & audiobooks by *K.J.Heritage* at the following stores:

Amazon & Audible, Apple, KOBO, Barnes & Noble/, Nook, Google, Smashwords & more

Links

Join K.J.Heritage's *Newsletter*

Get an inside track on all future releases, access to early reading copies (ARCs), sneak previews, and more.
http://kjheritage.com/join

Mastodon

@kjheritage@mastodon.online

Instagram

Photos of my wonderful Shollie rescue #RescueJack, piccies of my best mugs of tea, and various and shameless images of all my books. Oh and maybe yours truly on a good hair day!
https://www.instagram.com/k.j.heritage

Twitter:

90K+ followers
@kjheritage

TikTok

General silliness and book stuff. Search for #kjhtok
https://www.tiktok.com/@k.j.heritage

BookBub:

Not only can you check out the latest cool book deals, but you can also get an alert when I publish my next book
https://www.bookbub.com/authors/k-j-heritage

Goodreads:

Friend me here:
https://www.goodreads.com/kjheritage

K.J.Heritage Facebook Group: *Mostly Readers*
Fun chat and posts about reading… *mostly.*
https://www.facebook.com/groups/mostlyreaders

K.J.Heritage Facebook page: *Mostly Writing*
Follow/like and keep in touch with even more writery stuff!
https://www.facebook.com/mostlywriting/

Website:
http://kjheritage.com/

Email:
Want to get in touch? Well here's your chance
contact@kjheritage.com

About *K.J.Heritage*

"K.J.Heritage's uncanny sense of pacing and story puts him at the forefront of today's speculative fiction writers."
Samuel Peralta, Amazon bestselling author and creator of The Future Chronicles

K.J.Heritage writes books that he loves to read. From science fiction action and adventure mysteries to contemporary thrillers, comedy, and paranormal fantasy.

When he isn't penning third-person descriptions about himself, he's an international bestselling author writing the books he likes to read. From psychological thrillers and mystery sci-fi to crime, action & adventure, and epic fantasy. He should really stick to one genre, but he's not that kind of writer... or reader.

His first sci-fi short story, *Escaping The Cradle* was runner-up in the 2005 Clarke-Bradbury International Science Fiction Competition.

K.J.Heritage's short story CHURCHILL'S ROCK, part of the 'Chronicle Worlds: Legacy Fleet' anthology, will be aboard the Astrobotic's Peregrine Lunar Lander set for launch on the United Launch Alliance's Vulcan Centaur rocket platform bound for the moon in June 2022.

He has also appeared in several anthologies with such

self-publishing sci-fi luminaries as Hugh Howey and Samuel Peralta.

K.J.Heritage has done all the requisite 'writery' jobs such as driver's mate, factory gateman, barman, labourer, telesales operative, sales assistant, warehouseman, IT contractor, Student Union President, university IT helpdesk guy, British Rail signal software designer, premiership football website designer, gigging musician, company director, graphic designer, stand-up comedian, sound engineer, improv artist, magazine editor and web journo... Although he doesn't like to talk about it. *Mostly. Maybe a little bit.*

He was born in the UK in one of the more interesting previous centuries. Originally from Derbyshire, he now lives in the seaside town of Brighton. He is a tea drinker, avid Twitterer, and neurodiverse (ASD) human being.

FOR ALL media enquiries, event/booking information, signed copies, etc. please email: *contact@mostlywriting. com*

All the very best,

K.J.Heritage

Continue reading for a sneak preview of
Book Two, *Shattered Web...*

K.J. HERITAGE
INTERNATIONAL BESTSELLING AUTHOR

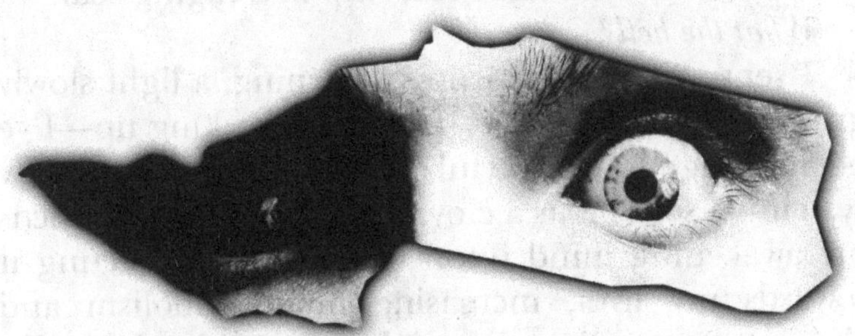

SHATTERED WEB

coffin

PRESSURE PULLING at me, flinging me up and down, straining against my arms, legs and back. Spinning me around. I'm trapped, unable to move—like I'm tied to the mast of a ship in a raging sea.

What the hell?

I sense my consciousness returning, a light slowly growing in the distance. This is not waking up—I've been drugged. A powerful sedative is squatting in my system—I sense it as a cloying, swirling cloud. I focus my awakening mind upon the narcotic, directing it towards my liver, increasing my metabolism and sifting the offending chemical from my blood. Finally, I'm able to force back the shroud of darkness and open my one remaining eye.

I find myself in a long, coffin-like box. But this is no burial, I recognise it for what it is... *a one-man escape pod*. I'm wearing my skinsuit, my breath magnified by a flimsy helmet.

Everything is fuzzy. Whatever narcotic has been used on me has temporarily affected my memory.

I twist around, releasing my arms, and I'm hit with a fresh burst of gees. The pod is on autopilot and struggling. I bring up the HUD and, within seconds, I've got the craft under control.

I pass my eye over the readouts and baulk at what I see. I'm in hyperspace—no one launches a pod outside of normal space, not unless you have a death wish. The conclusion is a simple one—someone wanted to get rid of me. I've been drugged, placed in a pod and forcibly jettisoned.

A beep on the com and a familiar voice. *"Judging by the way that pod is handling, you must be awake. Good, I was getting worried."*

A name slams into my frontal cortex. *Stranng.* And with that name, my memories come flooding back. The Company. Being snatched from my colony ship. The Zeta Karst labs and that goddamn lunatic, Frederix.

"What the hell did you do to me?" The answer flashes into my mind almost immediately. *Shereena.* The ship's over-qualified medic. She arrived at my quarters earlier—a smile on her face. I'd been too much of a sap to bother reading her. That's what you get when you trust someone. And, of course, I'm cursed with vanity. I was consumed by nervousness and excitement—who doesn't feel like that before climbing into bed with someone new? We were kissing and… she stuck a damn needle in my neck.

"I'm sorry," Stranng continues.

I'm not physically close enough to read his intent but I know the man well enough to realise he doesn't mean it.

"Orders from above. Some damn Company grandee, even higher than your pay grade. Seems like they know what a son-of-a-bitch you are. That's why we drugged you. To make sure you complied. I can't say I was unhappy to get out of that airlock you imprisoned me in. Nor to get you off my ship."

I'm used to tight spaces… who isn't? Even the

literal ones like the one I'm presently in. Ship and habitat living is mostly cramped, but I've suffered worse. All due to those damn internment camps I was forced to grow up in—before the Company and its rivals decided to ignore Earth's *Decree of Genetic Manipulation*. 'Internment Camp' was a pretty phrase for *prison*—and not that pretty. Where I spent my formative years with the other Skilled. Punishment for minor infringements was draconian. I spent days in the choky, a box hardly bigger than the ship I'm flying in. It made no difference that we were only kids, although I preferred it in there. To me it was a goddamn reward. I've always preferred my own company. No wonder I got into trouble so often.

"If the Company wants me dead, why not just kill me?"

"*That's the point,*" Stranng replies. "*The Company needs you to be very much alive. Although I don't rate your chances.*"

I take in the information with little emotion. "Okay, give it to me straight. Why am I in this flying coffin?"

"*Because only small ships can manoeuvre in hyperspace without breaking up. It's taken all my skill to get you this close. Everything was primed and operational in your pod before we booted you off the ship.*"

"Close to what?"

"*You're to dock with another vessel.*"

"In hyperspace? Are you insane?" The only reply is static. "What damn vessel?"

"*Widen your nav-beams.*"

I do as he says, and I'm surprised to spot a blurred,

fluid outline like an extended blob. All com-signals are compromised in hyperspace, yet I can tell it's a design I've never seen before. Smaller and compact. I'm closing in on it fast.

"That's Ariadne. Some kind of experimental warship." Stranng explains. *"The fore-runner for a new fleet. Or so they hoped. The ship cut all coms and launched itself into hyperspace an hour ago and refused every attempt to contact her. Space knows what's happening on board. But we received this message…"*

There's a crackle over the com and then I hear the tell-tale emergency call-sign of a vessel in trouble:

> *Mayday! Mayday! Mayday! This is the CS Ariadne. Urgent assistance needed. The ship has locked us out of all systems. Repeat. We are locked out of all navigational and control systems. Additional. Unknown agencies aboard have shot and killed—*

"Is that all? I don't get it. The ship locked out the crew? How?"

"Ariadne is a bioship. An organic computer is running the show over there."

"You mean they're playing around with bio-computing? That's supposed to be illegal."

"'Supposed' goes a long way with the Company. You Skilled were illegal once, remember?"

I laugh through gritted teeth. A bio-computer can mean only one thing—the goal for computer consciousness is still alive and the Company has only gone and put one in charge of a goddamn warship. Nice. And if you're gonna build an organic computer intelligence, look no further than the human brain. The only problem? *Humans are not that reliable.* It sounds like another mess of the Company's making, a mess that I'm not motivated to solve.

"And here's the rub…" Stranng continues. *"The Ariadne is heading for rival company space."*

I know the Company inside and out. There's no way they'd let one of their ships cross into competing territory. Especially something experimental with a cash value to the opposition. It's that which concerns the Company grandees who put me in this position. "I guess your orders are to destroy the ship before she crosses over to the enemy, yeah?"

"You've got just under two and a half hours, otherwise it's boom-boom time."

"What the hell am I supposed to do over there? I'm only one guy, even if I am a Skilled."

"I'm sure you'll figure something out. Your type always does. Perhaps they want you to talk the ship down? Who knows or cares? I just follow orders. I'm also to warn you that there may be rival agents aboard or even terrorists."

"Terrorists?"

"The Company has tried to keep what I'm about to tell you hush-hush. There's been a spate of high-profile assassinations over the last few months. Grandees and VIPs. Some say there's a new terrorist group responsible for what's been happening. They call themselves Neo-Dawn. And, as it happens, there was a VIP event on board the Ariadne before this ass-mess kicked off, so watch yourself over there. It's either a malfunction, sabotage or a full-out hijack. Either

way, you've one job and one job only. Stop the damn ship and pull it out of hyperspace." Stranng laughs down the com. It ain't a pretty sound.

"And what if I refuse?"

"You don't exactly have a choice."

"How did I know you were gonna say that? The Company must be desperate. The chances of successfully docking a ship in hyperspace are—"

"You're the resourceful type… so I'm upping your odds to one in ten."

"That optimistic huh?"

"I've never heard of it being done before and no skin off my nose either way. You'll find a programmed wafer stuffed down your skinsuit. See it as a goodbye gift."

"You're all heart."

"Remember, you've just under two and a half hours to get the job done. Midnight, ship's time. Or thereabouts. I'll leave it to the last second—you have my word on that. But you've got a bigger problem. You must first dock with the Ariadne to get aboard. Another reason why the Company chose a Skilled—a mere human wouldn't stand a chance."

"It's always nice to be wanted. Anything else?"

"Nothing much. The wafer also comes with a complete ship's roster. There's forty-three souls aboard."

"And that's it?"

"Maybe the Company isn't comfortable sending you any more info. Or maybe that's all they could manage in the time frame. Make the best of it. You'll be passing out of com range any moment. You'll be on your own." A pause. *"Good luck…. You're gonna need—"* A crackle and Stranng is gone.

"Thanks."

I take a look at the navicom. The blob of the bioship is getting nearer. I'll have to fly in close using sight rather than instrumentation. Stranng wasn't kidding when he gave me a one in ten chance. These pods are difficult enough to manoeuvre in normal space. I'm not sure my piloting skills will be up to the task. Luckily, I'm a whizz on the stick. If I'm gonna survive, I'll need a big slice of luck. I decide to shorten the odds. I increase blood flow to brain and hands and, immediately, I can hear the reassuring thump of my heart in my ears.

All ships in hyperspace create a wake around them, like the disturbed air behind any atmospheric vehicle but significantly worse. The closer I get to the *Ariadne,* the more wake I will experience from her. Any fluctuation that I can't account for will send me careening away—or even kick me back into regular space. Either way, my pod will break up instantly…

My fingers dance over the primitive control panel— making constant adjustments and realignments. I boost the engines and gently edge closer to my target, bringing up the pod's external camera and I see the *Ariadne* for the first time.

Stranng was right. She ain't a normal looking ship. The Company is all about cheap, mass-produced modules. Different components bolted together with no thought for aesthetics. The *Ariadne* is curved and stylish, although I'm too close to see all of her. The Snag Drive array is what surprises me the most. It spreads out from the *Ariadne* like the legs of a spider. I've seen this configuration before. It's not normally used on military ships. The array is too vulnerable to attack, although it's fast and the most stable design for hyperspace. I have no time for contemplation. No matter how pleasing she looks, the *Ariadne* is creating quite a wake. With no schematics, I'm blind—her docking bay could be anywhere. I slow my speed, allowing the *Ariadne* to pull my pod along behind her and, using only the view from the distorted camera feed, I search the smooth, elegantly proportioned ship for a way inside.

And there it is. The cargo dock. A small opening in her stern.

My heart lurches and I have to concentrate hard to reduce its insistent beating. Flying this close to a ship in hyperspace is akin to suicide. The only chance I have is to line up the pod, hit the engines hard and try to punch my way through *Ariadne's* swirling wake.

And if I should make it?

How in space am I gonna stop from crashing? Whether I get inside the cargo dock or not, this ain't gonna be pretty.

I work quickly with the navicom, superimposing the lines of the hyperspatial wake over the crackling camera feed. They ebb and flow—like storm waves slamming into a rocky cove. Every now and then there's a lull. A repeating pattern. It's what I'm looking for. I watch and wait, knowing I've only got one shot at this. I must hope my prediction of the next lull is correct.

My heart wants to beat faster again. This time I let it thump away, sending a signal to my adrenal glands to flood my bloodstream with the adrenaline I'm gonna need to make those precise, speedy manoeuvres.

The last wave in the repeating cycle swirls through hyperspace and I punch the engines. I'm slammed by many gees, the adrenaline giving me the energy and the power to keep my hands over the controls, while the *Ariadne* grows on the screen.

The docking bay is only a couple of hundred feet away.

I'm gonna bloody well make it.

I wait to the very last moment. The pod enters the bay and I hit the reverse thrusters, slamming me with even more gee. Lights swirl in front of me. I push more oxygen and blood into my brain and try to steer the pod to a stop.

Shit!

I'm going too fast. The inner hull of the *Ariadne* flies towards me and I smash right into it.

ariadne

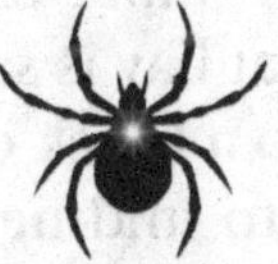

I PUSH my eye open and my mind is punched with a hard fist of terror mixed with pain, and something akin to madness. A swirl of out-of-control emotions trying to thrust themselves deep inside my mind. Invasive, powerful, and all-consuming. I'm under attack from another Skilled—but like no Skilled I've ever felt before. The emotions are too raw, too unhinged, and reckless. I bring up my wall just in time, the barricade I use to isolate myself from other empaths. It's a struggle. Like trying to dam an angry, storm-ridden sea. Somehow, I manage to push it back, to hold my ground. I slowly drive those feelings out of my mind until there's nothing left behind except a single word…

Ariadne.

I take a few calming breaths. I'm shocked but okay. I can still feel *Ariadne* pushing at me, but now those emotions are muffled and distant and I can see them for what they are. This was no attack, but a dreadful scream of empathic madness.

What the hell did the Company do here?

There is only one conclusion that makes any sense. *Ariadne*, the bioship's brain, is an empathic entity like me. *A Skilled,* or some distorted version of one, but broadcasting on a more massive scale.

I need to find out more about *Ariadne*, about what happened here. To do that, I'd have to let the ship back inside my head and that ain't gonna happen again soon. Not if I want to preserve my sanity. Besides, keeping her at bay is sapping at my strength. Like trying to hold up a block of crushing granite.

Strann gave me to midnight to solve this thing. I'm not sure I can resist *Ariadne's* powerful mind for that long. I now get why the Company wanted me aboard…

Using a Skilled to catch a Skilled.

Taking a few soothing breaths, I reassess the situation. I've still got a job to do and the quicker I do it the better. *Ariadne* or no. I force my mind to concentrate on where I am and what I'm doing. On the smashed pod's readouts—which are all flashing red.

I do a quick damage assessment of my own systems. No broken bones or internal injuries, although I have a lot of non-essential tissue damage. My helmet readout tells me my oxygen is in the amber. I don't have that long before my air is gonna run out. I need to get inside the ship asap.

Still… *I damn well made it.*

I imagine Strann's consternation. He can't know I survived but even his compromised readouts would tell him I got inside the docking bay. That's one in the eye for him. The bigger danger was from *Ariadne* herself. I doubt he knew what he was sending me into.

I jettison the pod hatch, helped by a few kicks, and drop heavily on to the floor. I'm still full of adrenaline and, behind its haze, I can feel a growing ache. No matter how much the pod protected me, high-gee impacts are not to be sneezed at. It's gonna hurt and hurt bad. I tune down my pain but not enough to numb myself. Hurt is a motivating force and besides, it's my early warning system.

I stand on shaky legs. I'm still emaciated after my time spent in hypersleep before Stranng 'rescued me'. I'm functional… just. I'm met by a scene of devastation. Two battered and smashed transports lie in pieces. Bits of their internal components scattered about the docking area like the aftermath of a tornado. One side of the bay is scored by the impact of my arrival. Where the pod slammed into it, I guess—now a crushed, battered mess. I'll say one thing for the Company, their escape pods are better designed than their ships. They're usually only accessible to those with suitable rank. Self-preservation is very important to the Company, for those certain, important few that is. Hence the advanced dampening field stopping me from being pulped by all those gees of impact.

The possibility of a ship crashing into the cargo bay is not one the Company or any organisation ignores. The inner airlock is accessible via a sturdy, blast and crash-proof bulkhead. This ain't no basic shield—it's covered with something I've never seen on a Company ship, a beautiful etching of a vast spider sitting within an intricate web. The ship I glimpsed from hyperspace.

Ariadne.

A goddess from Greek myth. She oversaw the sacrificial labyrinth wherein lurked the Minotaur. I'm no Theseus, that's for sure. If I have to slay a beast with the body of a man and the head of a bull, I'm sure gonna be pissed. In comparison to what the

Company has done here on this bioship, the myth of the minotaur is small beans.

If there's any monster aboard this ship, it's *Ariadne* herself.

I shake my head and enter the airlock. The heavy outer-hatch slides shut behind me. I punch the recycle. Nothing happens.

Huh?

I punch it again and still no reaction. There's no way the pod caused damage this far inside the ship. The airlock must've been shut down, deactivated intentionally. Alarm bells sound in my mind. With what happened with *Ariadne's* disturbed mind, I forgot what I was getting myself into. If I can't get inside the ship, I've no chance of solving what's beyond the airlock door and no chance at surviving longer than the air left in my suit.

I walk to the internal airlock door and peer out of the window, a small rounded portal. A young, petite female in fatigues—a Company ensign—lies on her back in the corridor beyond, like she fell where she was standing. I can't tell if she is alive or dead... but I don't hold out much hope. Her face is blotched, a bloated, purple tongue sticking out of her mouth like she's been strangled. If she hasn't perished, she soon will. My intuition tells me the girl was gassed by something nasty.

"What the fuck have you done here, *Ariadne?*" I whisper to myself.

Suddenly, getting out of the airlock and into the ship, doesn't seem like such a good idea any more. My skinsuit will protect me from any surface contaminants, but my air won't last forever. At some point, I'll have to breathe the ship's atmosphere.

The flash of shadows and two figures come hurrying into the outer airlock area, young kids barely out of their teens, wearing what look like low-ranking, ceremonial fleet personnel uniforms of white and orange although they're unfastened, sweaty and smudged. They carry rifles nestled into their shoulders, eyeing down the barrels and see me at once, the guns swivelling in my direction. I've nowhere to hide and do the only thing I can do. I shrug and raise my hands. I guess crashing my escape pod into the docking bay didn't go unnoticed.

One of the kids, short, sweaty looking with greased, slicked-back, black hair and equally greasy features, edges towards the airlock door and presses the com. "Who the hell are you? And how did you get aboard?" he blurts, an intense expression creasing his youthful face.

By the sublieutenant insignia on his cuffs, I guess he's the leader of this twosome. He's so short and stocky that his rifle is as big as he is.

The other kid stands tall and gangly at his side, sweat dripping down his face. He's a good-looking, short-haired blonde with striking, almost noble features. Intense blue eyes stare out of a face full of sadness and woe. Whatever has gone down on this ship has badly affected him. He wears the insignia of ensign, the fleet entry rank.

I realise they are just teenagers. They seem younger somehow. Maybe it's the fear etched into their faces. One thing is for sure, they don't look like hijackers. I drop my arms and patch my helmet into the airlock com. "You guys gonna let me aboard or what?"

The diminutive sublieutenant stabs his rifle in my direction. "I said, who are you? Answer the damn question!" His voice is no match for his words. Squeaky and stress-filled. He looks past me to see if I'm on my own.

"Who do you think I am?" I reply bullishly. "The Company ain't gonna let this ship fly away without sending in one of their top operatives. That happens to be me."

The kid looks confused. I try and make things a little easier for him. "Open the door! That's a direct order from your superior. Go inform the Strategist that I'm aboard. I want to talk to someone in charge, asap!"

The sublieutenant pulls back for a one-to-one with his blonde friend. While they chat, I take a guess that whatever went down on this ship hasn't helped their mood. Judging by their shaking heads, I'm betting they're less than keen about my arrival.

I want to try and read them, but that would let *Ariadne* back into my mind. And that's not ever going to happen. I can feel her madness crawling at the edge of my sensibilities, her tentacles writhing and probing. That would be suicide. I've become just as blind, just as ordinary as the next sucker—almost.

Another individual arrives in the airlock area. A tall, burly man in his forties, his skin light brown and greasy, with greying, curly hair that spills onto his vast shoulders. He wears the stained overalls of an engineer. He pulls up short when he sees me. I can tell by his shocked reaction that, even with my eye-patch and my one visible eye, he knows what I am.

"Who are you?" I ask over the com. He ignores me and strides over to the sublieutenant and joins in the discussion. His arrival results in more shaking heads and the flinging of arms. Disagreement. This carries on for some time until the big guy with the grey curly hair spins around and lumbers purposely towards the airlock. The Company grunts don't like this one bit. "Stand down, Hewlis!" the sublieutenant shouts, raising his gun.

Hewlis doesn't listen.

"I'll shoot!" the sublieutenant yells like a petulant child. "You know I will!"

The engineer raises his hands and stops, his lived-in eyes staring at me in apology. "The Company sent him here!" he rasps. "Can't you see that?"

"So, not everyone aboard this ship is an idiot," I say over the com.

"Shut your mouth!" the sublieutenant shouts at me.

"You gotta let him out, Drex," Hewlis pleads. "We need all the help we can get."

A low beep from my skinsuit helmet and the amber air readout flashes red. "If you don't let me out of here soon, I'm gonna run out of oxy—"

The greasy-haired kid, Drex, offs the com. What happens next is another intense argument, but Drex and his friend outnumber Hewlis two to zero. Two guns that is. Which will win most arguments. As for me, the result ain't that good. Hewlis doesn't want to give up without a fight, but it's as I said—guns always win out—especially if a pair of grunts wield them.

I don't get it? I hit the ship with quite a clunk. Why would the strategist send down a couple of green-ass low rankers and an engineer to go check it out? The answer ain't a palatable one. *The Strategist is dead or injured.*

Drex and the blonde kid escort a scowling Hewlis away.

The red flashing in my helmet becomes insistent.

Damn! The last thing I expected was to get stopped at the first hurdle. I'm hoping Drex and the rest have gone to find someone with more authority to sort this out. I have no choice but to wait. With my air running low, that ain't gonna be easy. But I ain't one of the Skilled for nothing.

I sit down, propping myself against the airlock wall, slowing my heart and respiration, closing everything down other than my vital systems. I can survive in a self-induced coma for an hour or two without oxygen. Not that this ship has that long. Hopefully, whoever's in charge will come get me before that time runs out.

I concentrate on my heartbeat—now a distant thud. Filling the time between each extended beat with small bursts of brain electricity. I leave the airlock behind and enter a deep meditative state…

vatic

SOMEONE IS slapping my face. I open my eyes to see Hewlis standing over me, his brown eyes flashing with concern. My heart lurches back into scudding action and quickly I throw up my wall. This time I'm ready for *Ariadne's* invasive and insane mind. It's still a struggle, but I push her quickly away. I take a deep breath of warm ship air. Despite any worries about gas or poison, I'm instantly re-energised. If there's something nasty in the ship's atmosphere, I can't smell it.

"Thanks," I say, pushing myself angrily to my feet, legs creaking with the effort.

"Don't thank me," Hewlis replies, towering over me like a bear. "I didn't open the airlock. You look terrible."

"I'll survive," I bark back at him, breathing heavily. "I'm Vatic. And that's what I'm famous for… surviving."

"Vatic." He repeats the word mechanically.

"Yeah, just Vatic. Don't overuse it."

Sublieutenant Drex pushes the tired-looking engineer aside. "How come you're still alive?" he asks, sounding disappointed. "Your suit was in the red."

"Like I said, I don't kill that easy. I guess it was you who let me out? Cos that was a good decision."

Drex shrugs, a confused expression on his youthful face. "Not me," he says, his voice an exaggerated squeak. "The airlock opened by itself. We thought you were dead."

I glance over to the sad-looking blonde kid. "What's your name?"

He points his rifle at me. "Ensign Murton Boyd." His voice is full of emotion. The kid is choked.

What the hell has gone down here?

I turn my attention back to Drex. "Just how fucking old are you both?"

"You can't talk to us like that!" he bleats.

"I'll talk to a little piss-ant like you any way I want. I haven't forgotten that it was you who left me in the airlock to suffocate to death."

Drex stares into my one, wired, manic-looking eye and I see that same flicker of recognition I've had all my life. "You… *you really are a Skilled,*" he says.

My eyes, like all others of my breed, have a certain *look*. Like we're on drugs. Manic almost. And even though the range of colours match those of regular humans, our eyes have an intensity that is difficult to ignore. Mine are a bright, wired, and startling blue. Although, I've only got one on show.

"Of course he's a Skilled!" Hewlis replies with exasperation. "I told you what he was. Not that you believed me. Who else could get aboard a ship during hyperspace and still be alive after his suit's oxygen ran out? They're a breed apart." He flashes his brown eyes in my direction. "No offence."

I shrug. "You'd have to try a lot harder to offend me." The issue with the airlock and who decided to let me out, can wait for now. I have far more important concerns. "Listen up," I say. "The *Ariadne* is heading towards rival Company space which means that if we don't stop her and stop her soon, we're all gonna go boom-boom." I'm using Stranng's words—I want to be sure the message gets across without any confusion.

The news hits Drex and his young friend hard. Hewlis grits his teeth, his grizzled lower jaw rising to form a grimace. Hopefully the information will focus their minds. I need everyone working together if we're gonna get out of this mess.

"What do you mean, go boom-boom?" Drex asks.

"Where do you think I came from? A puff of damn smoke? A Company ship is shadowing the *Ariadne* out there in hyperspace. I happen to know the Strategist in charge. He's got one hell of a twitchy trigger finger, you get me, Sublieutenant?"

Drex doesn't like being talked to like this, that much is obvious.

I pull myself up to my full-diminutive height and take a deep breath. "I need to know what's been going on here. You can start by telling me why there's a dead body outside the airlock."

"You're not giving the orders around here," Drex says, bristling as if this is a playground power play. "You're under arrest until I say otherwise. Skilled or not."

"And what gives you the authority to put me in chains?" I ask, aware of a cloying heat. Company ships are normally a lot cooler. No wonder Boyd and Drex are sweating like pigs.

"Our Strategist and all other senior officers are dead," Hewlis explains calmly. "Sublieutenant Drex here, is the only surviving fleet officer of rank." He raises his eyebrows at me in a way that says the kid ain't up to the job, but I can see that for myself.

"Dead?" I take in the information with an annoyed shake of my head. I'll find out exactly how they died later. First, I need to stamp my authority. "I'm taking command as of now," I say to Drex. "You get me?"

A relieved smile passes over Hewlis' ruddy face.

Drex shakes his head. "No way. You don't look like no Company Grandee to me. Where's your uniform? Where's your ID?"

I point to my one remaining eye. "This is all the ID I fucking need."

Drex ain't impressed. "You don't have the rank, you don't have—"

I slap the kid in the face.

Drex is shocked, his eyebrows furrowing, fingers tightening on his rifle.

I slap him a second time and a third, jabbing a quick elbow into his guts, and, with a twist of my other hand, his rifle is in my possession.

Boyd shouts, his gun now pointing at my head but he's uncertain.

"Like I said, I'm taking command." I slam the rifle back in to Drex's hands. "Attention, Sublieutenant!" I bark.

Drex stands there, motionless, a look of suppressed anger twisting at his face.

"Listen up! My name is Vatic, I'm a full member of the Secondary Executive, giving me authority over you, your warrant officer, your strategist, and the goddamn rear admiral of the Company fleet if it comes to that. Which means that when I say jump, you jump, you get me?"

Drex makes the wise decision and draws himself to reluctant attention—but I haven't broken him yet. In response, Boyd drops the rifle to his side and dutifully salutes. Like I've always said, grunts prefer someone with real authority in charge.

I push through them, exit the airlock, and go over to the body on the floor—the girl I spotted earlier. A blackened tongue sticks out of her mouth, like a frozen scream, her eyes wide open and staring with a look of terror—a clear sign of asphyxiation. Like I thought, she's dead. But even though her body lies outside the airlock, she hasn't died from depressurisation. There are no tell tell-tale skin blemishes—just blotchy patches. *A toxin of some kind.*

"How many other survivors?"

"Seven," Hewlis answers.

"Seven?" I turn towards him. "Out of forty-three?"

The engineer shrugs, his mammoth shoulders rising and falling in a practised gesture. "I guess so."

"You said the Strategist and the other officers are dead. Did they all die like this?"

Drex draws breath to speak but I'm still pissed at him for leaving me to die in the airlock. "Not you," I say. I turn my attention to Boyd, who seems a lot more relaxed about me being in charge. "What happened, kid?"

"It started a little over two hours ago," Boyd answers, tears forming in the corners of his eyes, his voice thick with emotion. "Twenty-hundred hours ship time. The air supply was poisoned. Some kind of gas, I guess, sir,"

"You sure that's what it was?"

Boyd nods, a distraught look crossing his face. "We were heading towards the Hospitality Suite on ceremonial duties for tonight's VIP party. You know the type of thing? Stand by the doors looking smart when…"

"When what, Ensign?" I bark.

Drex and Boyd swap glances.

"Out with it!"

"We were in the ship's elevator, sir," Boyd says. "It's off-limits, but… but we were late and thought it would be quicker than the stairs. We walked inside, the doors closed and… the thing got stuck between floors. When the elevator finally started moving again, we emerged to find everybody dead and a strange smell in the air."

The tears that were forming in Boyd's eyes, now drip down his cheek in twin streams. He wipes them away with the back of his hand.

"You okay, recruit?"

He nods. Whatever happened aboard the *Ariadne* has hit him hard. Maybe too hard. "The other survivors, where are they?"

"In Hospitality," Hewlis replies, the engineer's large brown eyes red with tiredness. "That's where we left them when Drex ordered me to try and break into the bridge with him and Boyd."

I take in the information with a nod of my head. Something doesn't feel right here. I remember the wafer stuffed inside my skinsuit and pull it free, tapping the screen into life. It's just as Stranng said, a roster of names and ranks—forty-three of them, and not more than a paragraph or two about each. Is this all I've been given to work with? ...Shit!

I glance at the time:

21:52

Two hours to midnight, give or take. To solve this thing. I wonder if I can last that long under the terrible assault of *Ariadne's* mind.

I access the roster again. The wafer tells me nothing extra about Drex or Boyd other than they're fleet low-rankers just starting out. Drex's promotion to sublieutenant was nothing special—regular career progression for a keen recruit. And Drex is the keen type, that's for sure.

I breathe deeply. The ship air is warmer than normal and smells stale with a hint of antiseptic—missing the all-pervading stink of sweat and piss. "What happened to the toxin?"

Boyd shrugs, pulling himself together. "Whatever was in the air dissipated, I guess."

"If everyone is dead, who's flying the ship?"

"No one is flying the *Ariadne!*" Drex blurts, unable to keep quiet. "The bridge is in lockdown and the security cams show everyone dead inside. That's why we've been trying to break in. We need to get back control as soon as possible, especially now that we know we're heading towards rival space."

"No one is flying her? Why would someone poison the crew and everybody else if not to gain control of the goddamn ship? And even if they somehow got access to *Ariadne's* nav-systems, why fly her to the

Company's closest rival? No enemy agent would be so stupid as to head for home. That'd be suicide, not without backup from other ships. They'd instead try and hide *Ariadne* somewhere out of the way."

"She must be flying on autopilot," Hewlis says and, even without my empathy, I can tell he believes there's more to it than that.

"We need to get back control of *Ariadne*," Drex says, before I can answer the engineer. "If there's another Company ship out there waiting to blow us up, that has to be our priority."

I take a deep breath. "Be quiet Sublieutenant. What you think is now unimportant. I've taken charge of this shit-show. We're doing nothing until I get a clear chain of events. I want to know what happened here. Step by step."

Drex looks like he might explode. I realise a few slaps ain't gonna be enough to get him in line. I turn to Hewlis. "You. Take me through what happened."

Hewlis nods, his lived-in eyes closing for a second. "The ship has been preparing for this evening's VIP function for a couple of days now," he begins. "Some swanky gathering to show off the *Ariadne*. We were in standard orbit around a Company planet. Awaiting arrivals."

"Who organised the party?" I ask.

"Professor Anil Chandrasekhar," The burly engineer replies with a curl of his lip. "He's the egghead behind the design of the whole ship. The *Ariadne* is his project, his design…"

"*CHANDRASEKHAR?*" *THE* name is unfamiliar.

I check the roster.

> *Professor Anil Chandrasekhar.*
> *Age: 162.*
> *Cereb specialist.*

Cereb. Short for 'cerebellum'—*brain matter*. And the *Ariadne* is a bioship. I can understand why the Company wants to use a human brain to run a warship, or more precisely, a Skilled brain. That at least makes sense. Even if what they have done here sickens me.

Computers developed exponentially in the early days of their construction, but the curve soon slowed and levelled. The result? Stalemate. When all your rivals have identical battle computers, no one has the upper-hand.

It was this stalemate that led to the companies investing in banned genetic manipulation. An illegal attempt to boost the human part of the equation. That's where I came into the story. Me and the other Skilled.

When Earth learned of what the companies were doing, that they were flouting 'Earth Law', their programs were shut down and the Skilled taken away to live out their lives in Internment. That soon changed after the Companies revolted. Earth lost its power to a conglomeration of vested interest. To turnover and greed. To a percentage calculation of profit over loss.

I can't be too bitter. It was that change that led to my freedom. And I admit it, in those early days, I loved the Company. I lived for it.

Until the inevitable war.

Without the balance of an independent Earth, the Companies ended up fighting over a fucking resource map, where the resources were suns, planets, moons, and entire solar systems.

The Company—*my Company*—was the victor... or at least it came out on top. Annexing Earth. Relocating its First Executive Board onto the home planet. But not without cost... The war was destructive. It's taken quite a few years for the Company to rebuild, to get back to where it once was. The other companies have also been busy. Borders have been strengthened and many warships patrol them. That's why *Ariadne* has come into being. This bioship must be an attempt to gain the upper hand, to end the stalemate forever. But whatever Chandrasekhar was trying to create here has gone gravely wrong.

"Chandrasekhar?" I say finally. "Is he one of the survivors?"

"He was the guest of honour," Boyd answers, wiping beads of sweat from his forehead. "He was expected to give a speech to the party of VIPs." Boyd's bottom lip trembles. "The last time I saw him was this morning. Arguing with the ship's Strategist again. The professor is now probably dead with everyone else."

I ignore Boyd's conjecture. "Arguing?"

He nods. "An ongoing thing. Those two have been at loggerheads for months now."

"Over what?"

"It's not my place to say."

"Just tell me!"

"Small things mostly. They didn't get on."

"And tonight's party? The *Ariadne* was in a stationary orbit—waiting for the guests to arrive, is that it?"

"I assume so," Hewlis answers. "But I'm an engineer not a maître d'."

"That's right, sir," Boyd continues. "The guests all arrived on board this evening. Ferried in by our transports."

My mind goes back to the smashed cargo bay and the destroyed ships, but I don't let myself get distracted. "Then what?"

"They were escorted to Hospitality. Just a straightforward Company gathering," Boyd continues as if he'd been to a few himself, although his expression tells me this was nothing like anything he'd seen before. "Guests, consorts, officers and a few waiters. Me and Drex were to be stationed by the door. Everything was normal until…" his voice dries, his eyes flicking over to the dead ensign lying on the floor just a few feet away. "Until everyone died."

"And you heard nothing about a murder?"

"A murder?" Hewlis says, his eyebrows rising to disappear behind his thick, curly greying hair.

"Let me explain," I say, fixing the burly engineer

with my one good eye. "Before the ship jumped into hyperspace, which I guess was before everyone was gassed, the coms-officer sent out a mayday. It said they'd been locked out of the ship, and that there had been a murder aboard. I don't know who the victim was… not yet, anyway, but I'm sure the two events are linked in some way. If I find who was killed and why, maybe I can make sense of this whole thing. So, let me ask you all again… did you witness anything out-of-the-ordinary before the gas attack?"

A shake of heads.

I stare back at the two low-rankers. "Have you searched the ship?"

Drex swaps a glance with Boyd. "What's the point?" he says with exasperation.

Before I can reply, a woman arrives in chef's fatigues, a thin, dark-skinned Hispanic whose expression shows intrigue at my appearance, slowing her steps as she notices me, before striding purposely over.

"What're you doing here?" Drex shouts, rounding on her. "I ordered everyone to stay put in the Hospitality Suite while we were attempting to get access to the bridge."

The chef eyes Drex with disdain. I can see from her expression that she's as impressed with the kid as I am. "Who are you?" she asks me with more authority than her displayed rank of Third Chef would suggest.

"I'm the schmuck the Company has put in charge to get to the bottom of this goddamn mess. What's of more importance is… *who are you?*"

The woman glances at Hewlis for confirmation.

He nods, widening his eyes.

"I'm Chef Velez," she replies, like the name should mean something to me.

"From the catering corps?"

"Yeah. Although I'm a lot more than a simple caterer." Her voice is all calm, yet I can see the fast beat of her heart in the twitch of her neck.

The woman possesses a peculiar beauty. Her eyes are slightly misaligned, her nose hooked and a little crooked, yet it works for her. She doesn't look or sound like a Third Chef Technician to me. Velez carries herself with the authority that comes from long experience of ordering people around. She's in her forties, making this exotic specimen too old for such a lowly rank. Third Chef translates to 'chopping duty', the job of a teenager or someone starting out. She's an enigma. Without my empath skills to help me, she could be hiding any number of sins.

"At ease, Velez. The cavalry's just arrived. Or haven't you worked that out yet?" I say.

She takes a few calming breaths and the twitching stops.

I tap at my wafer.

Jurado Velez.
Age: 46.
Company Designate: Third Chef Technician.

Holder of some quite impressive culinary awards. I read on. She was demoted from the top galley rank of Executive Chef, but there's no reason why.

"It says here you're a whizz with food? What the

273

hell did you do to get busted?"

Velez's green eyes stare at me, unfazed by the question, and I glimpse a fire within her.

"I upset the wrong person," she replies enigmatically. "I'm one of the best chefs in the Company and they did this to me." She points a knife-scarred finger at her uniform and sneers.

I carry on reading the wafer. There's a date for when she joined the *Ariadne* but since Stranng woke me out of hypersleep on that colony ship, god knows how many days ago, I'm out of my reckoning. "How long have you been aboard?"

"Two days. I requested the assignment. The more VIP functions I can cater for, the better my chances of getting my rank back," she says, although I'm not sure I believe her.

"How did you survive?"

"I was in the galley," Velez answers. "In the cold-storage area on my own with the door closed."

"What were you doing in there?"

"Despite my lowly rank," Velez spits, "I was still expected to work on my famous signature desserts. I am an artist who demands perfection, which means absolutely no interference. That's why I was inside and alone. When I emerged..." A frown crosses her features. "I found everyone dead."

I'm wasting time—I guess they all have a similar story—and decide to move things along.

"Okay," I say, addressing them all. "This is how things are gonna go down. First, I want to visit the bridge and take a look at that com feed for myself. Then I'm gonna head to Hospitality and interrogate the rest of the survivors. In the meantime, I require a head-count of everyone aboard the *Ariadne*. Dead or alive. And if they're dead, an assessment on how they died. The Company roster says forty-three souls aboard. If there's anybody else on this ship who shouldn't be, I need to know about it. If you find more survivors, take them to the Hospitality Suite. I'm gonna make that my temporary HQ." I turn to Drex and Boyd. "I want you two to take care of that."

"A head-count!" Drex fumes. "When we're racing towards enemy space? Are you mad? We should be trying to break into the bridge or disabling the Snag Drive. I don't care about who you are or where you're from, you ain't telling me what to do."

Apart from the rifle, Drex carries a buzz-gun on his waist. I step up to him, my face next to his. "Give me your side-arm, Sublieutenant!" He pauses in indecision, which is all the motivation I need.

I snap the gun from its holster. And, in one quick motion, pistol-whip him to the floor. "I'm not gonna ask you to do things twice… you get me?"

Drex is stunned, not from the actual blow—I didn't hit him that hard. I don't think he's ever been treated like this, which must come as a shock to the kid. It's the second time I've beat up on him and, I admit, I'm enjoying myself. I point the gun at his head.

"Don't you think I want to get off this damn ship just as much as everyone else?" I say. "With the bridge in lock-down, it'd take you days to breakthrough. Days we don't have. It's a waste of our time. The fact remains… *Ariadne* is heading for one big explosion in hyperspace in under two hours if we don't stop her.

The way I look at it, you either help me by doing what you're told, when you're told or… you're just as useless as this corpse and the others on this goddamn ghost ship. Believe me, at this point, I'm quite happy to let you join them."

My little performance is just that, a performance. If I'm gonna get these idiots out of this mess, I need to play hard and I need to play rough. There's no time for anything less. Would I shoot the kid? Maybe? Who knows? But self-preservation sure is one motivating force.

Drex nods.

"Say it!"

"Yes, sir."

"Good."

Boyd pulls Drex to his feet, a look of determination upon his grief-ridden features.

I take Drex's belt and holster the buzz-gun to my waist. "Get that roster back to me asap. Dismissed!"

Drex wipes his nose and he, and Boyd, quickly disappear into the corridors.

"That was a little rough," Hewlis says.

"You wanna make a complaint? Then I suggest you do it to the Company, when you get the chance that is. From this point on, you'll do what I say when I say it. You get me?"

Hewlis nods but Velez stands her ground. "What did you mean… *we're heading for an explosion?*"

I tell her about *Ariadne's* destination, and Stranng shadowing us in hyperspace.

Velez ain't impressed to say the least. "I don't like Drex or his friend," she says, the twitch returning to her neck, "but he does have a point. What will questioning the survivors achieve? If the priority is to get this ship out of hyperspace, aren't you wasting time?"

"The kid needed slapping down, don't make me do the same to you," I bark, wondering why it's so hard for this goddamn crew to follow orders.

"I just don't want to die," Velez continues. "Like everyone else."

"You want that kid back in charge?"

Velez shakes her head.

"Good. Cos I'm the only chance you've got."

Want more?
Buy it now!

http://books2read.com/shatteredweb

(full online store links for your country of residence including Amazon, Apple, B&N,

Google, KOBO and more)

www.ingramcontent.com/pod-product-compliance
Lightning Source LLC
Chambersburg PA
CBHW010539170726
48285CB00008B/2684